For eight long years Lee Martin had carried a bitter hatred for the Ashbaughs. They had burned his father off his homestead, destroying, in that one horrible night, both his parents' dreams. Now Lee had come back for vengeance—but it was turning sour in his mouth.

There was nothing left of the Ashbaughs. Old man Cleatis had died of a heart attack, and Newlin, Cleatis' son, was a weak, crippled man, confined to a wheelchair. Kate, Newlin's sister, had grown into a beautiful but trouble-weary woman.

Revenge? Lee thought bitterly. *There's no one left to fight.*

Then, one day, Lee found out he was wrong, and the country exploded in violence.

NEMESIS OF CIRCLE A

Giles A. Lutz

CHARTER BOOKS, NEW YORK

NEMESIS OF CIRCLE A

A Charter Book / published by arrangement with
the author

PRINTING HISTORY
Charter edition / June 1976
Fifth printing / May 1985
Sixth printing / April 1986

ISBN: 0-441-56924-2

Charter Books are published by The Berkley Publishing Group,
200 Madison Avenue, New York, New York 10016.
PRINTED IN THE UNITED STATES OF AMERICA

I

The calendar said that spring had arrived, but this high country didn't know it. Snow still remained on the north slopes, and the wind blowing over it had a bite in its teeth. The rider dug his chin deeper into the collar of his sheepskin coat. He wanted a smoke, but that would mean removing his gloves to roll a cigarette, so he decided against it. He rode stoop-shouldered, and weariness showed in every line. The horse was equally weary; it had no spring in its step, and the hoofs came up and fell with a dull heaviness. The long miles behind it gave it a right to its weariness.

Lee Martin leaned over and patted its neck. "Another half hour, Amigo, and we'll eat and rest." The horse snorted lugubriously and continued his plodding climb.

Lee thought of the flat Texas country so far behind him with a sharp nostalgia. Texas had been an easy-paced country with permanent warmth and sunshine, and in a sudden spasm of anger he cursed this high country. But all the years he had spent in Texas had been temporary, a stopgap until he could return here. He hadn't known the high country long—a little over a year—and he intended to leave it again as quickly as he could. It depended upon how long it might take him to do a job. Eight years was a long time to carry a hate, but whenever it dimmed he had only to remember a certain night with firelight flickering on cruel faces and the crying of his mother and sister falling on unhearing ears.

The road crested, and he looked at the valley below. He let Amigo blow after the climb, and the horse's labored breathing formed vapor clouds at his nostrils.

The sight of the town's lights below drove all thought of physical discomfort from his head. "River Bend," he said, hardly realizing that he had spoken aloud. A thousand times the name had flashed through his mind adding to the scar tissue already burned there. A river hardly big enough to be called one drove out of the mountains and bent slightly at the town's north side. His father had fallen in love with this country on sight, but then Harvey Martin hadn't known what had been ahead; he hadn't known about the Ashbaughs.

A moment before, the sheepskin hadn't been adequate. Now it was too warm. The extra warmth came from within him, from the fire of his hating.

He unbuttoned the coat and stripped off his gloves. He built a cigarette and fired a match. Its flame showed a harshly-molded face, the jaw line cut with rock severity. The Texas sun had laid its deep coloring on the skin, making the eyes a startling blue by contrast. It hadn't been able to touch the new-moon shaped scar on his chin. It was almost an inch in length, and it stood out starkly white against the darkness of his complexion.

The face was too young to be set so harshly. The lips looked as though laughter was unkown to them, and the eyes had a deep brooding. The nose was a hatchet blade giving sharp-edged assurance to the face. His frame was as lean as his face, and not an ounce of fat was wasted on his six feet.

He drew a last time on the cigarette, savoring the smoke filling his lungs. The sound of Amigo's breathing was easing, and he flipped the cigarette away. He watched the glowing arc until it crashed in a shower of sparks then asked, "You ready to move, Amigo?"

He buttoned his coat and drew on his gloves before he set the horse in motion again. The wind seemed to have picked up a new bite.

He said, "Amigo, if you're as tired of me as I am of you, you'll get down there in a hurry."

Amigo understood, or the downhill going quickened his stride. Lee spent the remainder of the way into town debating whether he wanted a meal or a drink first.

The town hadn't changed, unless a thirteen-year old's memory was at fault. He saw the same high-fronted buildings along its one important street, and if any of them had been painted during his absence they didn't show it.

He passed the general store and the saddler's. The three saloons were as he remembered them. Even the names on the store windows were the same. In eight years nothing had changed.

He saw Homer Iman coming out of the tiny office

sandwiched between a saloon and Kelly's barber and undertaker shop. A light streaming from the saloon reflected briefly from the badge on Iman's coat. This hadn't changed either. Iman was beginning another of his countless rounds about the town.

He moved less spryly than Lee remembered. Did eight years age a man that much, or did a kid look at the law with more awe in his eyes?

He kept his face averted as he passed Iman. Maybe the eyes had aged along with the steps, but Lee was taking no chance of Iman recognizing him.

He looked back after a dozen yards, and Iman hadn't paused. Lee's teeth flashed in a mirthless grin. Iman wasn't interested in a stranger riding down Main Street on a chilly night.

He pulled up before the livery stable and hesitated before he swung down. If old man Oakley was still alive this would be his severest test. For the old man had a remarkable memory when it came to horse or man flesh. It was said that once he had seen a horse or a man he never forgot either.

Lee shook his head in disgust at his hesitation. What difference did it make if Oakley recognized him? He wasn't afraid of the Ashbaughs finding out he was back. They would find out sooner or later. He had done the same thing with Iman; he had ducked his face to avoid being recognized. He had broken no law. He could shout his name until everybody in town heard it, and nobody could touch him. It was only that he had no definite plan and until he did he could move more freely if he wasn't known.

4

He led Amigo into the runway between the box stalls, and familiar smells assailed his nostrils. There was the good smell of hay laced by the stronger one of manure, more pungent now than usual because of the winter's accumulation. The weather must have been holding bad here for some time, because Oakley ran a clean stable and given any stretch of good days he would have attacked the manure piles furiously.

Oakley came out of his office, and Lee was shocked by what the eight years had done to him. He remembered him with kindness, for Oakley had never shouted at the kids for playing about his place.

Oakley shuffled to a stop and said, "Yes?" There was a querulousness in his tone, as though he hated to be disturbed even for business. His head was bent much lower, and the skinny neck seemed too fragile to support it. His old eyes were rheumy and they watered as they stared at Lee in a puzzled attempt at remembrance.

"Can you put him up tonight?" Lee asked.

"That'll be fifty cents. Don't I know you?"

"If you do you don't have to ask me. Give him some oats too."

"That'll be fifty cents more." Oakley shook his head as though giving up on this face. "You pick him up by six o'clock tomorrow night, or there'll be another charge."

Lee laid a silver dollar in the outthrust palm. "I'll pick him up or pay," he said shortly.

He felt a relief as he moved back to the walk. He should have realized the difference between a thirteen-year-old kid and a man. Just maturing would wipe away the softness and vagueness of a kid's face. And he hadn't belonged to anybody important. Most of these people had never known his name. When they wanted him for some reason they had referred to him as "Hey, kid." He could move about as freely as he wanted, and no one would recognize him.

He debated again upon the drink or meal, and the drink won. He headed for the *Three Deuces*. He needed that drink to drive the chill out of his bones.

He had never been inside the saloon before, but he had peeked through its doors as he had waited for his father. If it had changed he couldn't tell it. It had been a fascinating place to a kid, filled with male laughter sometimes harsh and ribald but always humorous and amused. He remembered a few breaks in that laughter when whisky had stretched tempers too thin. He had seen several fist fights and once a shooting. Harvey Martin had taken his hand after it had been over, and his face had been grave. "I'm sorry you saw that, son," Harvey had said. Lee had never found out what the shooting had been about.

He stepped inside, feeling no timidity. He had been entering saloons since he had turned eighteen. There was no difference in a Texas saloon or one in the high country. The furniture had an equal weariness, and the sawdust on the floor was as soiled in one place as another.

He didn't pause inside the door. That pause called attention to a man quicker than anything else.

A few heads turned to follow his progress to the

bar. Then the laughter and talk resumed. He ordered whisky, and the bartender filled the shot glass. He held it pointedly until Lee paid twenty-five cents on the bar.

"That right?" Lee demanded.

The bartender met the flash of temper in the blue eyes calmly. "That's right, mister." He moved along the bar, but he left the half-filled bottle in front of Lee.

The temper was gone. The bartender had a right to his suspicion; he'd probably learned it by long experience. A stranger shouldn't expect to walk in here, be served and not pay for it right away.

Lee threw the drink into his mouth, letting it hit the back of his throat before it slid down. He knew what kind of whisky saloons served strangers. His expectations weren't severe enough. The whisky was raw and green. He shut his eyes briefly against the gagging, and a shudder ran through him. When he opened his eyes the bartender was watching him, a cynical grin on his lips. The grin faded under Lee's blank stare.

He could give the whisky one credit: it had authority. It hit his stomach like a club and a bonfire couldn't throw out any more heat. Lee felt the warmth stealing through his body, erasing the chilled tightness of his muscles. He unbuttoned his sheepskin and pushed back his hat.

He looked in the long back-bar mirror. He could see most of the room in it, and it was half-filled with strange faces. Now that was Kimbrough who ran the general store over there, and McKinley talking earnestly to him. He couldn't give himself credit for McKinley, he thought: he had recognized the smithy more by size than by face.

Three poker games were in progress, and his eyes went uninterestedly over the first two. They stopped at the third game, and a burning stronger than anything the whisky made started in him. Four men sat at the table. and the big man facing him in the mirror was apparently losing. The irritation of it showed in the flush of his face, and it was helped by the liquor he drank steadily.

A harsh band tightened around Lee's breathing, and a roaring filled his head as he looked at that beefy face. There weren't enough years in his life for him to forget it. The last time he had seen it, firelight had been reflected from those small, pig eyes, and the mouth had sagged in a loose grin of animal pleasure. The scar on Lee's chin started an odd, tingling itching as though it too was aware of the man. It should be—the toe of Orrie Pratt's boot had made it.

The bartender said, "Are you all right, mister?"

His words broke the murderous impulse to kill Pratt where he sat.

A little sanity returned to Lee's eyes as he looked at the man. "All right?" he said thickly. "Why?"

"I dunno," the bartender said dubiously. "You looked kinda green around the gills, like you'd been looking at ghosts."

The man didn't know how right he was. "I'm all right," Lee said. For an instant he had teetered on a knife edge, and he could as readily have fallen off on the violent side. He intended to kill Pratt, but not at the moment.

He forced himself to look at Pratt's reflection in the mirror. Eight years hadn't changed Pratt much. The added weight only made him look more solid. He was massive through the shoulders and powerful of chest. He had a reputation for brutal fists. Some claimed he could break a man's jaw with a single blow.

Lee wondered if Pratt still worked for the Ashbaughs. He must, for he was still around. Lee had a list engraved in his mind. Cleatis Ashbaugh headed it, followed by his son, Newlin. When he had taken care of those two, then he would turn his attention to Orrie Pratt. After all the years of thinking about it he had almost upset his plans in that first, murderous flush.

Pratt lost another hand, and the three men at the table looked worried. Suddenly, Pratt seized the cards from the hands of the man who was shuffling them and threw them across the room. An uneasy silence fell on the room before the last card fluttered to the floor.

"Give me another deck of cards, Donny," Pratt roared. He poured himself a glass of whisky, and his face was savage.

The bartender didn't move fast enough to suit him, and Pratt lumbered to his feet. "Didn't you hear me? I want a new deck."

Donny moistened his lips. "Give me time, Orrie."

Pratt carried his drink with him, and his steps were

unsteady. A raw, red violence had seized his face. He was drunk and mean, and he wanted to take it out on somebody.

The space to Lee's left was open, and Pratt was heading for it. Lee didn't want Pratt standing beside him . . . for two reasons. First, he couldn't trust himself to be near the man. Second, Pratt might recognize him, and he wasn't ready for that. The best thing he could do now would be to clear out of here while he had the chance.

He picked the wrong moment to turn. Pratt veered his course, and Lee plunged full into him. He knocked the hand holding the glass of liquor up and back, spilling it over Pratt's shirt front.

Pratt stared at the stain on his shirt, then looked at Lee.

Lee mumbled, "Sorry." He didn't dare look at Pratt. What was in his eyes made a lie out of his apology.

A wicked glow shined in Pratt's eyes. "You're gonna be, you clumsy bastard. I'll show you just what sorry is."

Lee couldn't stand up in a fist fight with the man. He hadn't the power nor the strength. He could shoot him in the guts, and it was a tremendous temptation. But that would ruin everything. No, it had to be a fist fight, but it had to be ended as quickly as possible.

He backed until he felt the edge of the bar against him. He reached behind him, and his fingers grasped the neck of the bottle.

Pratt took the retreat as a mark of fear. A vicious

grin parted his lips. "Don't be scared, boy." He beckoned with his fingers. "You don't have to be scared of Orrie Pratt."

Lee lifted the bottle. The remaining liquor gave it satisfactory weight.

His lungs could no longer contain the words. "Come on, you sonofabitch. Come on."

The shock of it held Pratt momentarily motionless. Then he lowered his head and roared as he plunged forward.

Lee slipped to one side, avoiding those reaching hands. He raised the bottle with savage force and crashed it against the unprotected head.

It made a dull, sickening thud, and the bottle broke, leaving the neck in his hand. Pratt had bulllike vitality. He still moved forward, but his head was drooping, and his arms were sagging. The overhead lamp picked up the shine of wetness in his hair, and the shine slowly turned to pink. He crashed into the bar, and bounced off of it. He turned, and his eyes looked blind, but they still rolled in search of Lee. His hands were held belt high, and struggle as he might he couldn't seem to raise them.

"Goddam you," he said, and his voice sounded bewildered. He tried to take a step, but his knees unhinged, dumping him on his face. The pink ran down his cheek and puddled on the floor, strengthening in shade. Now it was a bright red and flowing hard.

"My God," an awed voice said. "Look at him bleed. He's killed him."

II

Lee tried to watch every man in the place. When the shock that held them trancelike wore off, some of them were going to do something . . . and he didn't know if that action would be for or against him.

He cursed the events that had led up to this, cursed the impulse that made him pick the *Three Deuces* saloon. This had marked him, and the very best he could hope for now was that his freedom of movement would not be curtailed.

He took a backward step toward the door, and men remained motionless before his baleful blue eyes. They read something ominous in them, read something in the hand dangling near the holstered gun. Anybody trying to stop that one would be taking a grave risk.

Lee continued his slow retreat. The door had to be near his back now, though he didn't dare turn his head to look. The room was still holding motionless. Evidently Pratt had few or no friends here tonight.

"Hold it," a voice behind him said. "And move your hand from that gun."

The authority in the voice froze Lee. He had forgotten all about Homer Iman and his rounds of the town.

Lee debated his action. He doubted Iman had a drawn gun, for he wouldn't have known anything was wrong until he had stepped inside. He could whirl and beat the aged marshal; he was certain of that. But if he did he would brand himself forever.

Iman was aware of the thoughts raging in the rigid figure before him. He saw it straighten and some of the tension flow from it.

"That's better," he said dryly. "Now turn around slow and hand me that gun."

Lee obeyed the first command. He looked at Iman's outstretched, empty hand. Iman still hadn't drawn. He had always been too damned sure of his authority; it was a wonder somebody hadn't blown off his head before now.

Those hooded gray eyes scrutinized Lee's face, taking it apart feature by feature, then trying to reassemble it in a familiar pattern. He didn't shake his head, but the gesture was there.

There was a tired grayness in his face, and a droop to his body. Men spoke of Homer Iman with respect, and Lee knew that as a kid he had looked at Marshal Iman with awed eyes. Then Iman had been nine feet tall. Now he was a tired, graying man with slowing steps.

He picked his gun out of its holster with a careful thumb and forefinger. Iman took it, looked at its well-worn butt, then glanced quizzically at Lee. His eyes knew a gun that was used and cared for.

He thrust the gun into his waist band and said, "Now somebody tell me what the hell's going on."

A dozen voices tried to speak at once, and Iman roared them into silence. "Goddam it. One at a time."

"He busted Orrie's head," McKinley said.

Lee couldn't detect any regret in the smithy's voice.

"I got eyes," Iman said acidly.

"It looks like he killed him."

"He's still bleeding," Iman said practically. "Somebody better get Doc over here before he bleeds to death."

A couple of men ran out of the door, and Iman's eyes singled out the bartender. "Donny, you better give me the straight of it."

Donny pursed his lips in thought. "Well, I'd say Orrie was at fault." Heads bobbed in agreement all around the room. "The stranger was minding his own business," Donny went on. "He turned to leave and bumped into Orrie. Orrie was drunk and mean. He picked the wrong man."

"What'd he hit him with?"

Donny glanced at the shards of glass on the floor. "A bottle. About half filled. Somebody's going to pay for that whisky."

Iman allowed himself a frosty grin. "I'd say it was spent in a good cause." He looked at Lee. "Come on."

"Where?"

"To jail."

"Damnit," Lee raged. "You heard the bartender. He started it. What did you expect me to do—just stand and take it?"

Iman's face was patient. "Maybe you broke his head clean through. If he dies that makes it a different matter. I'll have to hold you until we see what happens."

Lee said bitterly, "He started it, and I go to jail."

"He's going to jail too as soon as his head's patched up."

Lee stared at him. "You said I busted his head."

"I said maybe," Iman corrected him. "I know Orrie Pratt's head. No bottle is going to break it. But I've got to hold you until I'm sure."

Something that Harvey Martin had once said came back to Lee: *Old Homer's stubborn, but he's honest. He goes ahead just as he sees it, and he don't care how many toes are in the way.*

Some of the bitterness left Lee. Iman was going ahead just the way he saw it.

Iman nodded brief approval, and Lee thought resentfully, *Those damned old eyes could look at a man's face and read his thoughts.*

"Let's go," Iman said.

He stopped at the door and looked back. "I'll be back after Orrie. You tell him that, in case he's got any other ideas."

He shut the door behind him and stepped up even with Lee. They didn't speak as they covered the block to the jail. As they walked inside the small building housing the office and jail, Iman said, "If Orrie's all right I'm not even fining you."

"Thanks for nothing," Lee snarled.

"I thought that might take some of the tightness out of you. What kind of a load are you packing, anyway?"

His face didn't change at Lee's silence. He looked as though he hadn't expected an answer.

Lee didn't think the office had been swept since he had left. One of the desk's legs was broken off, and a brick propped it up. The old chair listed drunkenly to one side. The kerosene lamp cast a poor light, leaving shadows in the corners. Its chimney needed cleaning and the wick needed trimming. Iman had spent almost a lifetime in this sad little office.

He moved aside for Lee to enter the cell. The door squeaked rustily on its hinges as he closed it. "Blanket's clean," he said. "I washed it last week."

He peered through the bars at Lee. "Sure seems I ought to know you. What's your name?"

"Sam."

"Lots of Sams in the world," Iman said mildly. "What else do you use to identify yourself?"

His lips twitched at Lee's silence. "It'll come out," he said softly. "Everything does."

As he started to turn away Lee said, "I haven't eaten yet tonight."

Iman nodded and continued on without breaking his stride.

He came back a little later with a beef sandwich and a cup of coffee. "Best I could do tonight. I had trouble arguing Alma out of this. The *Pearly Gates* was closed. That's a hell of a name for a restaurant. Every time I say the *Pearly Gates* is closed I feel like it's some kind of a prophecy against me."

He handed Lee the sandwich and coffee, and Lee took an experimental bite.

"You don't have to worry. That Alma's a good cook."

Lee nodded. The beef was good, and piled thick between the bread. It wasn't going to satisfy his hunger, but he wasn't going to starve either.

"I'm going after Orrie now. Doc ought to have him patched up."

Lee watched him wordlessly.

"I think Orrie's going to have a headache and a grudge. That doesn't touch you, huh? It would if you knew Orrie." He walked out of the office and closed the door behind him.

He came back a few minutes later, and he had Pratt by the arm. Pratt's steps were unsteady, and his words were incoherent.

"Sleep it off, Orrie. You'll feel better in the morning." Iman unlocked the cell next to Lee's and shoved Pratt into it.

Lee heard him stumble across the enclosure and flop onto the bunk. It creaked under the punishment.

Iman said, "Thought you'd like to know Doc Parker says he's got a split scalp. No permanent damage. Does that disappoint you?"

Those keen old eyes kept probing at Lee's face, trying to find a soft spot. "I guess it doesn't. I talked to Donny. After things settled down he remembered better. He said you kept staring at Orrie in the mirror, and he never saw so much hating in a man's eyes."

"He drinks too much of his own whisky," Lee said.

"Not Donny." Iman's face hardened. "I don't

know who you are or why you're here, but if you've got a crazy idea in your head like killing Orrie you'd better get it out."

"I could have killed him in the saloon."

"Not without paying for it. And I don't think you want to pay for it that way. I've seen a lot of men carrying a grudge. All it does is eat them up until there's nothing left." Iman waited a moment, then sighed. "It's a funny thing, but a man makes the road he rides on. He can make it a hard road or an easy one. Remember that."

He turned and walked to his desk. He steadied the chair before he sat down.

Lee stared at his back. He had ridden a hard road ever since he had been thirteen years old. And none of it had been his making. That terrible night came back to him as vividly as though it was happening now. He relived every minute of it—the terror, the outrage, the wild, helpless anger. . . .

Harvey Martin straightened in his chair. "Thought I heard something," he muttered. He was a big man, bending under hard, unremitting work. Those huge, clumsy-looking hands had skill in them and also a tenderness for his family. He saw the flash of fear in his wife's eyes and tried to laugh it off. "I'm probably imagining things."

Lee sprang up from the floor before the fireplace and raced to the rifle in the rack beside the door. "If it's that ole Cleatis Ashbaugh skulking around I'll run him off."

Harvey said sharply, "Let that rifle alone. I've told you before."

Lee's ten-year-old sister laid down the doll she had been crooning to. "He thinks he's growed up," she scoffed. "If ole man Ashbaugh made a face at him he'd run like crazy."

"I would not," he said fiercely.

Martha Martin said, "You two stop that wrangling." Remnants of beauty remained in the tired patience of her face. It had been a hard year, but the one-room cabin had been finished a week ago, and maybe now the press of work would slacken. She had worked as hard as Harvey helping build it, and there was pride in her eyes as she looked around the room. She had insisted on two things, a real floor and a big fireplace, and she hadn't let Harvey talk her out of them.

She said, "Harvey, do you think we could have a house warming? It would be nice to have a few friends in."

Then she realized her husband wasn't listening, and terror returned to her eyes. Cleatis Ashbaugh claimed no one would ever homestead his land. The government said it wasn't his land, but the government was far away, and Ashbaugh was here.

"Thought I heard old Rowdy yelp," Harvey said. "Maybe I'd better take a look around."

"Nobody better hurt my dog," Lee shouted.

"Quiet," his mother said.

Harvey moved to the rack and cradled the rifle in

his arms. He didn't fool anybody. Some inner tension strung him tight and made his cheeks hollowed.

"Harvey," Martha cried.

"It's nothing," he soothed her. "I just want to satisfy myself."

Lee was right behind him as he opened the door. The full moon bathed the land, but it was a cold light. Harvey stepped outside, and a loop snaked out of nowhere, dropped around him and pinioned his arms to his sides.

A moment before, there had been emptiness; now the night seemed suddenly filled with menacing figures. Lee's heart bounded up into his throat and lodged there as he looked at the horsemen.

Orrie Pratt said, "That's no hospitable way to greet us, meeting us with a rifle thataway. Maybe I'd better learn you a few manners."

He set spurs to his horse, and the rope snapped tight, dragging Harvey off his feet.

Lee heard his mother's shrill scream, and it broke the trance of his horror. "You let my Paw alone!" he shouted.

He rushed at Pratt and clawed at his leg. "Damn you!" he sobbed. "Damn you!"

"Another one I got to learn something," Pratt grunted. He lifted his boot out of the stirrup and kicked. The toe caught Lee full against the chin. Pain exploded in his head with a blinding burst of light. His mother's screaming filled his head until he thought it would burst with it. It broke off on a high, tearing note, and he knew nothing more.

When he came to, he was floating on a sea of pain. His lower face felt swollen, and it throbbed unbearably. He touched a hand to it and felt the wet stickiness on it. He couldn't understand what had happened to him, and he couldn't understand all this light. He closed his eyes again, and it came back to him a painful piece at a time.

He forced his eyes open against the sickness it brought him. The cabin and shed were on fire. Already flames had engulfed both structures, and their timbers groaned under the weakening onslaught.

Three horsemen sat watching the fire. Lee would never forget how Pratt's eyes gleamed by it. Off to one side his mother had her arms about Linda, and she was crying quietly. Linda wailed, and the sound was shrill and piercing.

Harvey Martin sat on the ground, his head bent between his knees. They must have dragged him a lot, for his clothing was in tatters and the dark smear of the earth that stained his upper body had a wet shine to it. Lee had to think about that shine until he realized it was blood. Harvey wasn't trying to fight them; he wasn't doing anything. He just sat there like something had been broken and he couldn't move.

Old Rowdy lay at the fringe of the firelight, his head a shapeless thing. Lee looked at him a long time before he understood. Rowdy had age on him, and his hearing wasn't as good as it used to be. They had slipped up on the dog and bashed his head in—probably with a rifle butt.

Lee got stiffly to his feet. The hurting locked his

teeth, and he forced his steps to be steady. He walked to the three horsemen. He looked at Pratt, but he meant it for all three of them.

"Someday I'm going to kill you for this."

"Why you little bastard." Pratt swung his foot free of the stirrup. "This time I'll kick your head off."

"Let him alone," Cleatis Ashbaugh ordered. It wasn't done out of pity, for there was no feeling on that old, hard face. A kid simply wasn't worth bothering with.

"I saved your team and wagon for you. You're lucky I didn't take your lives. Now hitch up and get out of here."

Lee had to do the hitching. His father's face was vague and formless, as though all comprehension had escaped him. He helped his father into the wagon bed and watched him stretch out in it. He wished his father would say something, but he didn't make a sound.

There was nothing to pack. It was all consumed in the fire. Martha and Linda climbed up onto the seat, and Lee picked up the reins. The cabin was swaying now, and in a few moments it would be a fiery pile of ashes. Lee didn't want to stay to see that.

He looked at the horsemen before he lashed the team into motion. He made a vow then, a vow that never weakened through eight years.

He wished his mother would cry. She sat beside him staring mutely ahead. It was far worse than Linda's wailing.

They drifted for months. Harvey never found a place that quite suited him again. His surface wounds had long ago healed, but the wound of the spirit wouldn't mend. He looked like a whole man, but he was only a shell. The insides of him were gone.

He died two years later, and Martha wore herself out trying to do for the family. Lee was drawing a hand's wage when he was fifteen, but there never seemed to be quite enough money. He knew his mother was dying years before it actually came. He guessed she had started dying the night Harvey had died. He stayed in Texas until Linda was married and secure. Then he was free—free to collect a long over-due bill from Cleatis Ashbaugh.

He gripped the bars with an intensity that made his hands ache. The ache brought him back to reality, and the old past faded.

You're wrong, Iman, he thought fiercely. *You're wrong when you say a man makes his road. He has no choice at all. One's picked out for him, and he's forced on it.*

III

Lee stretched out on the bunk. Pratt was moaning and cursing. None of his talk made sense, and Lee guessed at best he was no more than semi-conscious. Pratt was sick once. Lee heard the retching sound, and a sour, acid smell filled the air. It was going to be hell trying to sleep with Pratt next to him.

He was wrong. He fell asleep almost immediately.

Angry voices awakened him in the morning. He could tell by the slant of the sun's rays through the high, small cell window that the sun had climbed a long way.

"Get me out of here, boss," Pratt said. "I'm sick." He stood clutching the bars as though he needed the support.

"Shut up, damn you," a furious voice said. "I've had enough trouble because of you."

Lee knew that voice. It had been eight years since he had heard it, but he knew it. He swung his feet carefully to the floor and walked to the front of the cell. He expected the waves of hating to flatten him, and it was a shock that he didn't feel much of anything. Cleatis Ashbaugh was much smaller than he remembered him. But there couldn't be any mistake. That was Cleatis standing before Iman's desk. His face was lined and tired, and he looked sick. His color was bad, and if he wasn't shaking he gave the impression of it. Only the eyes were the same. They blazed with the same old virulence.

Iman said, "You got in earlier than I expected. Somebody must have ridden their butt off to let you know."

Ashbaugh made an impatient gesture. "Let him out. I've wasted enough time already. And I want the saddle tramp that did it held."

"What for? For protecting himself?"

"Goddam it," Ashbaugh roared. "Nobody hits my foreman without—"

"Without nothing," Iman interrupted flatly. "And you get Orrie out when you pay his fine. Fifty dollars."

Ashbaugh looked as though he would choke. He had poison in his eyes, and it was dripping onto his tongue.

"Watch what you say," Iman warned him. "Times have changed a little, Cleatis. You're not the big dog in the valley any more. And you don't make the laws."

He stood and put his nose not six inches from Ashbaugh's face.

Lee could see only the back of Iman's head, but he could imagine the glare on his face.

Ashbaugh choked on his rage, and color ran high in his face. He yelled, "By God, I've taken a lot from you, Homer. I'm warning you—"

Iman said in a suddenly weary voice, "Pay his fine, Cleatis. Or get out. I'm tired of talking to you."

Lee looked at Ashbaugh's face and thought, *He's going to explode*. Things had changed a little around here. He couldn't remember anybody ever daring to talk to Ashbaugh like this. Or maybe Iman always had, and Lee just hadn't been around to hear it.

Ashbaugh had to fight his breathing to get enough air to ask, "Will you take my check?"

"Cash," Iman said firmly.

"Goddamnit, the bank doesn't open for a half hour."

"I know what time the bank opens," Iman snapped. "Now will you get out of here and let me get some work done?"

25

Ashbaugh's breathing had a thin, reedy sound. "I'm going to live to see you out of office. I'm going to work on it. Next election—"

"Sure," Iman said wearily. He didn't look up as the door slammed behind Ashbaugh.

A blank wall was between the cells, and Lee couldn't see Pratt's face. He wished he could.

Pratt called, "Homer, one of these days you're going to push him too far."

"I don't want any lip out of you," Iman snarled.

Pratt shut up.

Lee gave Iman reluctant credit. He had stood up to both Ashbaugh and Pratt. Evidently he was a man entitled to respect.

Ashbaugh came back a half hour later, and he had a stack of bills in his hand. He counted out fifty ones on the desk, taking a deliberate time with it.

"I asked for ones," he sneered, "because I didn't think you'd recognize anything any bigger."

Iman's voice was jerky in an effort to control his anger. "Take him and get out."

He walked to Pratt's cell and unlocked it.

Ashbaugh stood before Lee's cell staring at him. "So this is the saddle tramp who's caused me so much trouble. I've got some advice for you. Get out of town before Orrie bumps into you again. Next time—"

"There won't be a next time," Iman snapped. "I told you to get out."

Pratt followed Ashbaugh out of the office. Lee watched them until the door closed. Ashbaugh wasn't a fearful figure any more. He was just a vitriolic old man choking on his own temper.

The estimate of the man had lessened—the hating hadn't.

He asked, "Are you going to let me out?"

"In a little while," Iman growled.

He waited almost an hour before he unlocked the cell. He stood in the doorway blocking it, and his eyes were gimlets boring deep. "I don't suppose you'd listen to some advice."

"Depends on what the advice is," Lee drawled.

Iman shook his head helplessly. "I've got a feeling about you. You want big trouble. You stay away from Pratt. You hear me?"

"And if he doesn't stay away from me? What do I do then?"

Baffled anger was on Iman's face as he stepped aside.

Lee said, "You forgot my gun."

Iman dug it out of a drawer and handed it to him. He watched Lee slide it up and down in the holster several times. He didn't miss the dexterity in those fingers.

He said flatly, "You kill him and you'll spend a lot longer in here. And I don't give a damn what the circumstances are. You remember that."

"Sure," Lee said.

He stopped at the door and turned a mocking face towards Iman. "Did I say thanks for the hospitality?"

He didn't push it further. Iman had a dangerous glint in his eyes.

That beef sandwich had been recommendation enough; he looked for and found the *Pearly Gates*. It was a clean little place with a half-dozen tables before the counter. Each table was covered with a red-checkered cloth, and Lee looked at one of them curiously as he passed it. It was clean. He couldn't remember seeing a clean tablecloth in a restaurant for a long time.

He sat down at the counter, and the woman asked, "What'll it be?"

Her liking for her own cooking was apparent, and she had a beaming humor on her full, round face.

"Fried eggs, ham and potatoes. About four eggs."

Her eyes danced with pleasure. She liked a man with an appetite. "You're new around here, aren't you?" she asked as she broke eggs into a frying pan.

"Just got in last night. I liked your cooking."

She turned puzzled eyes on him. "I don't remember you."

"Iman brought a beef sandwich to the jail."

Her face went still. "Oh," she said weakly.

He hadn't had to tell her that, but some perverse humor had prodded him. Anger returned. He didn't give a damn what these people thought of him.

It was an excellent breakfast. Alma kept darting furtive glances at him, and she didn't speak again. He had spent a night in jail, and to her that meant association with violence. She didn't want anything to do with him, and that suited him fine.

He strolled out onto the street after he finished. The sun was up full, and its warmth was the promise that a laggard spring was finally here. The snow on the north side of the roofs was melting, and he heard the constant drip, drip from the eaves. Spring was the time of the year most eagerly looked forward to in the high country. Cattlemen would be looking anxiously for the new grass, thinking of their winter-gaunted cows. And all the work stopped because of winter's white blanket had to be resumed. A man drove furiously in the few warm months allotted him just to begin to catch up.

He stood for a moment watching the traffic flow down the street. Wagons deepened the ruts already in the street, and if the ground firmed before a rain those ruts would stay most of the summer. People gathered on corners, discussing the work ahead, and women moved from one store to another hunting needed items.

The blacksmith shop was particularly busy. A half-dozen horses and four wagons were around it, and the ring of the anvil had a lusty sound. The smithy would be in a rush for several weeks as men brought in tools and equipment that needed repairing for the new season.

Everybody seemed to have a purpose, a destination, and it gave Lee a left-out and lonely feeling.

He tried to shake off the somber mood as he moved down the walk. He had a purpose too, and the remembering of it should have brought him more satisfaction.

Donny was sweeping some trash off the walk as Lee approached the *Three Deuces,* and his eyes widened. He stopped and with broom in hand blocked Lee's passage.

"I wouldn't go in there," he said, and there was some sort of earnest appeal in his eyes.

Lee had no intention of going in. It was too early in the morning for a drink, but Donny's warning put a perverseness in him.

"Why not?"

"Cleatis and Orrie are in there. I know you don't want any trouble with them."

"Do you?" Lee said, and brushed past the man. The perverseness intensified. He wanted that drink.

He looked back as he entered the door. Donny stood his broom against the wall and moved fast in the opposite direction. Donny was going after the marshal.

Lee stepped inside, and the room was shadowy after the brilliance of the sunshine. Pratt and Ashbaugh sat at a front table, a bottle between them. Maybe they had ordered Donny out, or maybe just them being here made the bartender uncomfortable.

They were arguing about something and for a moment they didn't see him. Then Ashbaugh's head swiveled around as though drawn by some irresistible attraction.

His face went mottled with color, and his breathing turned hard and raspy.

"What do you want?" he demanded.

Lee leaned against the wall and rolled a cigarette. His deliberation was an affront to an impatient man.

"Did you hear me?" Ashbaugh shouted. "By God, you answer me when I ask you something."

Lee's eyes traveled over him, adding to the insult. "When you got a right to ask me something then maybe I'll answer it."

He felt a wicked and dangerous malice course through him. Maybe this was the spot he was seeking. He would even push on it a little to help it along.

Pratt growled something and started to rise. Ashbaugh caught his arm and hauled him down. "Wait. He's after something. Look at him."

He stood and took a couple of steps towards Lee. "Who are you? What do you want?"

Lee blew smoke through his nostrils. and his eyes continued their insulting probing.

Ashbaugh's temper was at the explosive stage, and when it blew it would break his face into little, raw pieces. "Damn you," he shouted. "Do you know who I am?"

"I know."

The indifference of the acknowledgment made Ashbaugh choke. "I knew you were after something." The words came hard, as though it took tremendous effort to say them. "I'll find out who you are. I'll have Orrie beat it out of you." He lurched a little and threw out a hand towards a chair. He looked bad.

Lee came off the wall. "If he comes at me again I'll kill him." He thought he heard the door open behind him. He didn't look around.

"Why Goddamn you—" Ashbaugh started. His

voice rose steadily, then broke off on a high-pitched note. A grayness rolled across his face, washing all color from it, and his eyes turned back up into his head. He clutched at his chest as though he were trying to dig out some hurt there, and his features turned doughy and shapeless.

He tried to cry out, but his shaking lips wouldn't form the words. He wanted desperately to say something, he wanted to move, and he had no control of anything. He crumpled suddenly, as though every bone in his body had melted.

Lee found a trembling in his hands. He had seen men die before, but always as a result of violence, and the heat of emotions made their dying less terrible. This death had stalked in here without warning, and its terrible efficiency left a man limp.

Iman rushed past Lee and knelt beside Ashbaugh. He rolled him over and yelled, "Get Doc Parker. Quick."

Donny turned and flew out of the door.

Lee could have told Iman that a doctor was useless. One look at Ashbaugh's face should have been enough for anybody.

"What happened?" Iman's eyes went from Pratt to Lee.

"He came in here and started an argument with the boss," Pratt said.

"You're a Goddamned liar."

Pratt's eyes swung to Lee, and they looked startled. But the expected objection didn't materialize in them.

Ashbaugh's way of dying had taken something out of him.

"He just dropped dead, Homer. I'm telling you, it was a hell of a thing to watch."

Iman looked at Lee, and Lee nodded. Pratt's statement just about covered everything.

Doc Parker rushed in, carrying his bag. He was a rotund, short man with a grave face. A few drops of sweat glistened on his bald head.

His examination was little more than a brief scrutiny.

"Did he get in an argument about something?" he asked.

Lee and Pratt both nodded.

"I knew it would happen," Parker said, and he was talking to no one in particular. "I told Cleatis a hundred times if he didn't control his temper that bad heart could carry him away." He looked sorrowful, and Lee couldn't imagine anybody feeling too sorry at Ashbaugh's death.

"Somebody's got to tell Kate," Parker muttered.

"Orrie," Iman commanded. "Get out there and bring her back as quick as you can."

Parker added a further order. "Break it easy to her. This will hit her hard."

Pratt nodded and moved heavily toward the door. He put a dark glance on them before he plunged outside.

Parker said, "I'll go tell Kelly to pick up the body." He added almost in apology, "There's nothing I can do here."

33

Three men stood near the dead man, and none of them looked at him. Donny twisted his hands nervously, and Lee knew he wished Kelly would hurry. But business would be good tonight as men discussed Ashbaugh's death. Donny could sell a new round of drinks everytime he said, "He died on his feet. Right there. I'm telling you, it scares a man to see something like that."

Iman put fierce eyes on Lee. "Are you satisfied now?"

Lee hadn't had a damned thing to do with Ashbaugh's dying. If it came to a matter of placing blame, Iman had a part of it. He had started arguing with Ashbaugh earlier this morning. But Lee knew he could argue a week and not change Iman's opinion. His implied accusation wasn't worth denying. He had something else on his mind that dug at him. Kate Ashbaugh! He hadn't really thought of her in years.

IV

Ashbaugh's funeral was held the following afternoon. The crowd listened respectfully to the preacher's oration, and Lee wondered how many of them felt real sorrow. Not too many, he thought, for Ashbaugh had been a ruthless man driving to his own objectives regardless of who was hurt.

An open grave was beside and Lee had trouble

reading the faded letters on the headpiece. Kate's mother had lain there for many years, and now Cleatis was rejoining her.

The preacher was having trouble finding laudatory things to say about Cleatis, and he dwelt on how big he became, of how much land he owned and how many cattle he ran. But the words had an empty ring, for right now bigness like that didn't mean a damned thing. It had all been wiped out, and Cleatis Ashbaugh wasn't any bigger than anybody else buried here.

Lee kept his eyes on Kate Ashbaugh. She stood straight and proud, and she showed no signs of breaking. She wore a black silk dress, and her face was veiled. He wished he could see her face. He remembered a lot of things now that he forced himself to. He couldn't say he hated all of the Ashbaughs—this one he could never hate. If he remembered right, she was a year younger than he was, and she had sort of fastened onto him the first day he'd gone to school. She had stopped the kids from jumping the newcomer in a gang by saying, "If you've got to fight him you fight him one at a time." Even a twelve-year-old girl could carry weight—if she was an Ashbaugh. Lee had done all right, fighting his way up through four kids. Curley Middleton had stopped him, but Curley had been older and heavier. Even then Lee had fought like a wild, crazy one. Curley had had to put him down three times, and there had been awe in his face as he had watched Lee try to drag himself to his feet again.

"I say he's all right," Curley had shouted, and the fighting had been over.

He had been accepted by the kids a lot earlier because of Kate. And he had been grateful for all the lumps she had saved him. But she had embarrassed him by her attentions, and he had used to yell at her to quit following him. He remembered how her eyes would turn big and round with reproach as she dropped back. But the next day she would be following him again.

She would ride over while they were building the cabin, and she had brought fresh milk and eggs—priceless things. Cleatis had never known about those secret visits. Lee and Kate had been partners in a conspiracy, and it had made its own bonds.

The old scenes faded, and they had no weight against everything else that had happened. He stared at the willow slenderness of her. Kate was a woman now, and she wouldn't remember those earlier incidents. He felt a nostalgia he couldn't quite place.

The preacher said his last word, and the box was lowered into the ground. Kate stayed until the first shovelful was tossed in, and that almost broke her.

Lee saw her shoulders quiver, then Pratt took her arm and turned her. Lee looked around again for her brother. He hadn't seen Newlin at any time during the services, and that was odd—unless Newlin was no longer in the country. The thought brought its sense of disappointment and hardened his face.

Kate's and Pratt's course would take them within a couple of feet of Lee. He stood planted, and he had no worry about her recognizing him. She wouldn't even see him, just as she didn't see all the other faces that were here.

She didn't stop, but she hesitated. The veil hid her face, but he got the impression of a fleeting, questioning scrutiny. Then she moved on, and he knew the impression was ridiculous.

He turned to follow in their wake, but Homer Iman blocked his path. The stubbornness in his face said that Lee couldn't just brush by him.

"Did I break some law by coming here?" Lee asked angrily.

"What's your interest in the Ashbaughs?" Iman asked bluntly.

Lee waited until the last of the onlookers trailed by. He was aware of the curious glances each one threw his way. Iman's attention was marking him.

"Didn't I show enough grief to suit you?" he snapped. "I didn't see many tears."

Iman's face was set in the familiar, stubborn mold. "I saw you watching Kate. First it was Orrie, then Cleatis, and now it's her. If you've got any thought of doing her harm—" He breathed gustily and didn't finish.

"Get off my back," Lee said harshly.

Iman had control of himself again. "All right." His tone was quiet enough. "But I've got files and a memory. I'll place you before I'm through."

Lee shrugged. "Good hunting," he said, and pushed by Iman.

He went down the path leading toward town, and he

felt the impact of Iman's eyes on his back every step of the way.

He rode out to the Circle A three days later. He had allowed a decent interval to blunt the edge of her sorrow. He wished he could separate her from the rest of them, but her name made it impossible. When he brought harm to Newlin and Pratt he would involve her, but he couldn't help it.

He noticed the run-down condition of the ranch. Or had eight years made a change in his outlook? To a thirteen-year-old kid from a poor family, anything above him was riches. But he remembered Cleatis Ashbaugh's place as a shining example of a well-run ranch. Now he saw signs of untended decay. The sign with its big CIRCLE A hung by one chain from the archway over the road leading to the house. The lane was fenced on both sides by split rails, and in places they had tumbled to the ground. All of the fence was sagging, and he frowned at it.

The house and outbuildings added to the shock. The house needed painting, and the barns and sheds had a weary, listing look. Appearances said the Circle A was making a losing fight for existence.

He rode to the back of the house and threw off. He stood for a moment before he approached the house. He had the feeling somebody was watching every move he made.

He knocked on the door and heard the light patter of footsteps. His face was blank though his heart had picked up a queer beat.

Kate Ashbaugh opened the door. Oh yes, he remembered her, but not like this. The little girl had grown into a beautiful woman. She was tall, the crown of her black hair reaching to the bridge of his nose. She had the same gray eyes, but maturity had deepened them. He didn't expect laughter from her now, but he remembered a child's easy capacity for it and he wondered if the years had pressed it out of her. He hoped not, for it would be a loss.

She said, "Yes?" and those eyes never left his face.

"I was wondering if you could use another hand, ma'am. I know it's a bad time. I heard about your loss in town."

She said, "Come in," and held the door open for him. "We'll talk to my brother about it."

He controlled the savage twitch that wanted to seize his face. So Newlin hadn't left the country.

He said, "Yes, ma'am."

"What's your name?"

He faced her squarely and said, "Sam." He needed a last name to put with the one he had given Iman, and he added, "Sam Dennis."

He watched for any telltale sign that would say she knew the name was false. Nothing appeared in her face, and he felt relief. She didn't know him.

"Sam Dennis," she murmured and stepped ahead of him.

She led him into the big living room, and a man sat before a fireplace. Its crackling flames took the chill out of the room.

"Newlin," she said. "This is Sam Dennis. He's asking about a job."

The chair turned, and Lee stared in slack-jawed disbelief. Newlin Ashbaugh sat in a wheel chair, and a blanket covered his legs. His face showed he had come through a bad time. The flesh had wasted from it, leaving the cheeks hollowed and the eyes fevered bright. Once he had been a big man, but now only the frame remained. Whatever sickness he had had taken the rest of him. Lee put him somewhere near thirty years old, but he looked a dozen years older.

A faint flush appeared in Newlin Ashbaugh's face at Lee's staring, but when he spoke his tone was level enough.

"I don't know," he said slowly. "Orrie's been taking care of the hiring."

"Are you satisfied with it?" she demanded, and some passion put heat in her voice.

Newlin made a helpless gesture, and it included him and the wheel chair. It said, what can I do?

She answered that gesture. "You can hire Mr. Dennis."

She saw some remote fear touch her brother's eyes, and she said, "If Orrie doesn't like it, tell him to go to hell."

Lee stood in the middle of some family fight, and he didn't know what it was about. But he did see a woman taking over a job that was too big for her.

The weakness of self-pity crumbled Newlin's face. "All right," he muttered. "Do as you please."

He whirled his chair and stared fixedly into the flames.

She led Lee back to the rear door and said crisply, "You're hired, Mr. Dennis. That's the bunkhouse. Orrie and the others won't be in before dark. If he objects to my hiring you, tell him to see me."

Lee couldn't forget that crippled man in the chair. Something more than his body had been broken. His spirit had been broken too.

She guessed at his thoughts and said, "He was hurt over two years ago by an outlaw horse. Doc Parker said he would never walk again. Newlin believed him."

Lee forgot that the crippled man was an Ashbaugh, that he had earned that wheel chair. All he could see was a man chained for the rest of his life to the confines of a room. The horror of it coursed through him, and he said fiercely, "He ought to keep trying."

For a moment her eyes rested on his, and there was some kind of an appeal in them. "Yes," she said simply.

He put himself under control and said, "I'm grateful for the job."

She nodded without speaking.

He looked back before he entered the bunkhouse. She still stood in the doorway, and her loneliness seemed to reach out to him.

He walked into the bunkhouse and took a rear bunk with a rolled-up mattress. Twenty bunks were in the long structure, but only seven of them were made up. The Circle A's work force had been drastically cut. It was further proof of a losing fight.

He unrolled the mattress and heard a knock on the door. He stepped to it, and Kate handed him blankets and pillow.

She said, "I hope you like it here."

He said a harsh, "Yes," and turned away. He was here under a false name and false intentions. He was here for an entirely different reason than she suspected, and he would not let pity change his course. Cleatis and Newlin Ashbaugh had murdered his father and mother as surely as though they had shot them the night of the fire. The Ashbaughs had wiped out their hopes and dreams, and without them they had died. Nothing was ever going to make him lose sight of that. But who was he going to war on? Cleatis was dead, and Newlin was a crippled wreck. But there was still Orrie Pratt and the Circle A. That was enough to keep in mind.

He stretched out on the bunk and adjusted the holstered gun to keep it from gouging him in the leg. He suspected he would need it before the day was over.

He stared at the ceiling with blank eyes. He was here, and he still had no clear picture of what he would do. Anything that would hurt the Circle A would suit him, and something would turn up. He was here on the grounds, and he would recognize opportunity when it showed itself.

He heard the thud of many hoofs just before sundown. He didn't move, but there was a tensing in him. That would be Pratt and the hands.

He heard their rough talk and laughter as they unsaddled, then they came trooping into the bunkhouse. Orrie was in the lead, and he broke off in the middle of a sentence.

He stared unbelievingly at the figure on the bunk; then his face heated.

"What the hell do you think you're doing?" he shouted.

"Lying down." The tone of Lees' voice was insult.

For a moment it set Pratt back then he said, "Why Goddamn you."

Lee swung his boots to the floor. He still looked easy and unconcerned. He had never seen a harder-faced crew than the one behind Pratt. Their eyes were bright with an evil expectancy. Orrie Pratt didn't take that kind of talk from anybody.

"I'm working here," Lee said. "Miss Ashbaugh hired me this afternoon."

"You're a Goddamned liar," Pratt shouted.

"Don't ever say that to me again," Lee snapped.

One of the men behind Pratt said, "He's got a fat mouth, Orrie. Do you want me to pound it off of him?"

Pratt shook his head. "That's my pleasure," he said, and started forward. "When I get through with him she won't recognize him as the man she hired."

Lee sprang to the middle of the aisle between the bunks. The gun was in his hand before his boots touched the floor. His draw had been fast and deadly fluid, and it put a gaping surprise in their faces. He could thank the old Texas Ranger and two years of hard practice for his skill. At the end of the two years the old Ranger had said worriedly, *You're faster than I ever was. Some men got an instinct for handling a gun. I only hope I didn't go wrong developing it.*

Lee said to them, "You try to touch me, and I'll gut-shoot you."

Pratt licked his lips. He looked at the menacing gun and remembered how fast it had showed in that steady hand. He turned his head to the men behind him and yelled, "Go on. Rush him."

Lee grinned mirthlessly. "Sure, rush me. I've got five shots. Two of you will be left on his feet. Unless I get lucky and get two of you with one shot. That'd only leave one."

The men looked at each other, and one of them protested, "Hell, Orrie. We didn't bargain for no gun-slick in our own bunkhouse. You rush him."

Pratt cursed them, and he had a good command of oaths. They stirred uneasily under the lashing, but none of them moved a boot.

"I'll see about this," Pratt raved. "I'll see who's doing the hiring."

He turned and ran out of the door.

One of the men rolled a cigarette and licked it until it was damp. He had to fire three matches to light. He was a little, wiry man with eyes set so close together that at first impression they looked crossed.

"You done lost your job, Mr. Big."

"Maybe," Lee grunted.

"You have," the little man insisted. "Kate listens to everything Orrie tells her. I wouldn't be surprised if one of these days she marries him."

It was a profane statement, profane in its implication. Lee wanted to slash the man across the face with the gun barrel. If Kate felt that way about Pratt he should be glad to hear it. It would clear away a lot of confusion.

Pratt came back, and no thunder cloud ever looked as black as his face.

The men questioned him about his results, and he raved, "She says he stays. She's lost her Goddamned head. I'll make her change her mind." He raged until he ran out of breath.

Some of the sick disgust faded in Lee. The cross-eyed man had lied. Kate didn't do everything Pratt told her.

"Supper's ready," Pratt growled finally. Before he left the room he stabbed a finger at Lee. "You watch your step," he warned. "You watch every Goddamned step you take."

"I'll do just that," Lee murmured.

He followed the others to the long table set in the kitchen. It was a silent meal. Pratt looked as though every bite choked him, and he kept darting murderous glances at Kate. Newlin sat at the head of the table, and he didn't eat a half-dozen mouthfuls. Lee hadn't noticed that twitch in his hands earlier in the afternoon. Some strain was stringing Newlin fine.

It looked as though only Lee enjoyed the meal. Kate must have cooked it all, for he saw no evidence of another cook. It looked as though the ranch was cutting every corner it could.

He was the last to leave the kitchen, and Kate followed him outdoors. She asked, "Is everything all right?"

He said with bleak humor, "I wouldn't take any popularity contest with them. In fact I've been thinking of sleeping outdoors. It might be safer."

He saw distress in her face. "I didn't think Orrie would take it like this. Maybe I made a mistake . . ." Her voice faded.

He asked bluntly, "Do you want me to leave?"

Her chin firmed. "No. I don't. Will you sleep in the house until Orrie gets over being mad?"

He thought about it, then nodded. "I think I will. And thank you." He didn't know why his voice should come out so gruff.

He had no possessions in the bunkhouse, so he didn't go back to it. He lay in Cleatis Ashbaugh's bed and stared at the ceiling. This was the last place he had ever thought he would be. Nothing had turned out as he had expected. Every step he took only carried him deeper into confusion. He could see one mild ray of humor so far. Pratt was probably congratulating himself, when the new man didn't come back, that Kate had fired him. Lee was almost smiling when he went to sleep.

V

Gig Hearns said, "Orrie, you did a lot of cussing last night for nothing. When he didn't come back after supper I told you he'd lit out."

"You Goddamned fool," Pratt snarled. "His horse is still in the barn."

Hearns gulped and said a weak, "Oh." He turned the problem over in his mind then asked, "Then where did he sleep?"

Pratt controlled his desire to swear at him. Hearns had never been known to be heavy on brains. "Probably in the house." He couldn't keep the worried note out of his voice.

Hearns looked startled. "Hell," he said uncertainly. "She wouldn't let no ordinary tramp hand sleep in the house. Or would she?"

That was the point worrying Pratt. Who was this stranger? And what was his connection with Kate and Newlin Ashbaugh? Whatever it was, it seemed to have enough strength to afford him unusual privileges.

Hearns said, "Orrie, do you think he's from the Cattleman's Association? Do you think she asked for him because—"

Pratt grabbed him by the shoulder, and his fingers bit deep. "Why don't you scream it so everybody can hear?"

"Hell," Hearns said in aggrieved tones. "I wasn't

talking loud." But his eyes swept uneasily around him. "Do you suppose what I said is right?"

"I don't know," Pratt said grimly. "But I'll damned sure find out."

He stared off into the distance while his mind picked at the problem. He had spent a lot of sleepless hours on it last night, and he was no nearer a solution.

Hearns shifted uneasily beside him, and his presence irritated Pratt.

Pratt said, "Go on in. I'll be in in a minute."

He leaned against the porch railing, his eyes bleak. Would Kate dare hire some damned detective and set him after him? It was a disturbing thought, a thought that blackened his face. He'd have to watch every step he took until he was certain of where he was going.

His eyes were bleak as he looked back into the past. She had been eleven years old when he had first hired on at the ranch. He had treated her with a tolerant humor, the way a man would treat a harmless nuisance. She had followed him around and gotten in his way, and most of the time his patience with her had held steady. Besides, she had been the boss's daughter, and he had never forgotten that.

By the time she had been fifteen his indifference to her had vanished. No man could have overlooked the swelling beneath her shirts or the tight way she filled a pair of britches, particularly when she swung into a saddle. He had never dared look at her too long or directly. Cleatis would have pistolwhipped him off the place.

She wasn't a kid any longer; she was a woman grown. And he wanted her. It was a cumulative desire built up over the years, and sometimes he had thought he would burst with it. How many sleepless nights had he spent thinking of her? When a man got stuck on one woman no other woman could help him. He had proven that. When the frustration had been too bad, or he had been drunk enough, he had picked up one of the saloon girls in River Bend. He had used them brutally, enraged because they weren't the woman he wanted, so that now they practically ran when they saw him coming.

He swore in his throat, a soundless moving of his lips. Things had been working out just as he had planned until this new man had come along. Pratt's hands ached with the intensity of their balling. First Newlin had been hurt, and then Cleatis had had to cut down on his activities because of his bad heart. More and more of the actual management had fallen on him, and his lucking finding of the unknown passage out of the valley had shown him the way he could force Kate to turn to him. He had weeded out the old riders, the ones loyal to the Ashbaughs, and replaced them with men who followed his orders. It hadn't been hard to get rid of the old riders. He had been on them constantly until they had packed up in disgust and quit. Cleatis hadn't questioned him about it. Cleatis had just been relieved to have the trouble off his shoulders.

Pratt had picked the men he wanted, the ones who would follow his orders. He managed a tight-lipped smile. Why shouldn't they? He gave them a cut of every head that was stolen from the Circle A. He had gone into it timidly, stealing a few head here and a few head there. Success and lack of supervision had emboldened him. Newlin had been helpless, and the punch had gone out of Cleatis. Cleatis had raved and cussed at each new reported loss, but he hadn't ridden out to see what could be done about it. He had sat in the house, his dull eyes watching things fall down around him. Kate had tried, but a woman couldn't take care of two sick men and know what was happening on the range too.

Cleatis' death had left Pratt's road wide open——until this new man had come along. Pratt had been sure Kate was solely dependent upon him, and now she had hired this stranger. This wasn't the usual run of saddle tramps. He was a hard man, capable with his hands and a gun. Pratt had seen proof of both.

A couple of the men passed Pratt, and Ronders asked, "You skipping breakfast, Orrie?"

Both of them had curiosity in their faces, and Pratt growled, "I'll be in in a minute."

He had built so well and carefully, and now his final success was threatened. The Circle A was in trouble with the bank. Kate had to turn to him. It wouldn't be hard to convince the bank that he could save the ranch. And the bank would be willing to let him try. The bank didn't want the land right now. It was holding too much of it as it was.

His face was harsh and bitter as he considered all angles. Maybe he had gone too fast, and Kate had turned suspicious of him. But he had been so close to holding the ranch right in the palm of his hand. One final blow could wipe it out, and the agony of further waiting blackened his face. But he'd have to wait until he found out who the new man was and what he was here for.

He pushed off of the porch railing and went in to breakfast.

Kate said, "Good morning, Orrie."

He thought there was a new, searching quality in her eyes, and it was an effort to put a smile on his face. "Morning," he muttered in return.

He dropped into his chair and glanced at this Sam Dennis. Dennis was looking squarely at him, and Pratt switched his eyes. For he knew his hating was in them naked and open for all to see. He couldn't let it show too much—not right now, anyway.

It was a strained meal. Newlin never ate nor said much. The food was tasteless to Pratt, and he gave up trying to force it down. Every time he raised his head, Dennis' eyes were fastened on him. Goddamn him, he thought savagely. I'll fix him. Wait until I get him away from the house. There would be a thousand opportunities, and he picked at them in his mind. He breathed faster as one developed. He could do it right here in the barn before they ever rode out for the day's work. A quick club's blow on the head while Dennis saddled, and it'd be done. He could report mournfully to Kate, "I warned him against fooling around with Lobo. But he was so damned cocksure he could handle him."

It might even be a good touch to press a horseshoe into the wound. And who'd be able to say it hadn't happened that way? Hearns and any of the others would swear that it had happened just the way Pratt reported it. Iman would be out asking his usual questions, and he wouldn't be able to prove a thing.

He looked again at Dennis, a hot blaze in his eyes. Dennis was a dead man. He just didn't know it.

Hearns said, "What's wrong with you, Orrie? Usually you eat your plate."

Pratt cursed him under his breath for calling attention to him. Dennis had a sardonic weighing in his eyes.

He was glad when the meal was over. Kate had some sort of preoccupation in her eyes. He didn't wait for her to lay out the day's work. It had been a long time since she had done that.

He debated upon asking Dennis out into the barn, then decided against it. No; he would wait until he came out on his own accord. The more natural this looked the better it would be.

He caught Hearns' arm as they left the house and pulled him to one side.

He said, "Gig, you guessed right about him," and nodded solemnly.

Hearns looked startled. "Guessed right about what?"

Hearns never held an idea for long at a time, and Pratt said patiently, "He's from the Cattleman's Association all right."

"Oh my God," Hearns whispered. Panic was starting in his eyes. "Are you sure?"

Pratt's voice roughened. "No need to lose your head. I was sure when you first talked to me. But I was afraid you'd give it away at breakfast. After you fell asleep last night I prowled around. I heard him talking to Kate. She doesn't know anything for certain yet. She just got him out here to check around."

Hearns' panic was picking up speed. "We'll go to the pen, Orrie. If we kill him they'll just send another one."

Pratt's fingers bit into his arm. "Not if his dying looks natural. Who can help an accident?"

Hearns' breathing was raspy. "What kind of accident?"

"Lobo could kick his head off."

Hearns still didn't get it, and Pratt said impatiently, "I'll get his attention when he comes into the barn. Then you can break his head with a club."

Hearns' eyes brightened. "It could work. We'd blame it on Lobo. Everybody could say he fooled around Lobo after you warned him."

Pratt had been doing some thinking on that point. "Maybe it'd be best if it was just you and me, Gig." The more people involved the more shaky a position became.

Hearns grinned as he caught it. He nodded and said, "We can control our stories, Orrie."

"That's it," Pratt grunted and led the way to the barn.

The others were saddled, and he sent them on their way, inventing the first task for them that came to mind.

He looked around the barn. Light filtered in through some missing shingles, and the pungent smell of last winter's manure filled his nostrils. The barn needed a thorough cleaning. He'd run this place a hell of a lot better when it belonged to him.

He picked up a broken piece of wagon tongue and hefted it. It would make a brutal club. He handed it to Hearns and said, "If you miss I'll kill you."

Hearns' face was tight, and his eyes burned like hot coals. "I won't miss," he said huskily.

Pratt placed him beside the partition of the stallion's stall. Lobo fretted at their presence and lashed out a hind hoof. It boomed resoundingly against the wooden wall. The horse had a well-known and vicious temper. Pratt had wanted to kill it a dozen times, but Cleatis wouldn't let him. Right now he was glad Cleatis had stopped him.

He took a few steps and looked back. Hunkered down that way and in shadows, Hearns wouldn't be noticed unless he moved. *He better hadn't move,* Pratt thought savagely.

He fiddled around just inside the barn's entrance, and he thought Dennis would never come. He worked himself into a rage imagining what was happening. Dennis and Kate were talking, and he wished he knew what they were saying.

He risked a peek outside, and Dennis was coming

toward the barn. He ducked back inside, and his breathing was racing in triumphant anticipation.

He stepped back and waited until Dennis came through the doorway. He moved out and said, "Dennis."

He didn't miss the way Dennis whirled around or the startled twitch in his face. This Dennis reacted fast. Pratt erased the small worry in his mind. Gig was smart enough not to give Dennis much time to react.

He put a smile on his face and extended a big hand. "Dennis, I was all wrong last night. I admit it. As long as you're going to work here there's no sense in us being at each other's throats. We won't get anything done that way. You pull your weight, and I won't have anything more to say."

He was sure he said it with the proper degree of solemnity, but Dennis' face didn't relax. He had the coldest eyes Pratt had ever seen in a man.

The smile became a little strained, and his hand wanted to sag. *Goddamn him*, Pratt raged inwardly. *How much does it take for him to let down his guard?*

"Sure," Dennis said flatly, and those eyes belied the acceptance in the word. He didn't seem to see the proffered hand. "Don't push on me, and maybe I won't push on you."

His expression didn't change, but there was a shine in his eyes as though he enjoyed some secret joke.

Pratt lowered his hand. Before he could speak another resounding boom echoed through the barn. It was followed by a shrill, savage whinny, and the sound of pawing hoofs. Each hoof made a distinct thud as it was driven into the earth.

Pratt didn't look around. Lobo sensed Hearns' presence outside his stall, and it was driving him wild. Pratt's eyes gleamed. When that stallion got in this kind of temper it took hours to calm him down. This was working out just fine. After Hearns struck Dennis down all they'd have to do would be to drag the body in front of Lobo's stall, unlock the door and get out of the way. Lobo would come storming out of his stall and dance all over Dennis. Lobo would try to stomp the hated man smell out of existence, and after he'd put all those hoof marks on Dennis nobody would be able to say what had happened.

Dennis jumped at the first boom, then quickly identified the following sounds. "Sounds like you're keeping a bad one in there."

"A real bad one," Pratt agreed. "Nobody can do anything with him. For some reason Cleatis wanted to keep him around." He shrugged. "I don't know what Miss Kate will do with him now."

He watched Dennis narrowly. A horse like Lobo was always a challenge to a horseman. Dennis would walk over to that stall on his own.

"Never been rode?" Dennis asked.

"Never," Pratt answered. "And you keep as far away from him as you can." Oh, he was whetting Dennis' curiosity to a fine edge. He could see the sharpened shine of it in the man's face.

"Is it all right to look at him?"

Pratt considered it, and his face was dubious. It was difficult to keep the malicious laughter from his eyes. He had wasted a lot of thought considering how he would get Dennis over there.

"I guess a look won't hurt," he said doubtfully. "We built a stall for him that'd hold an elephant. Even then I wouldn't say Lobo won't break out of it some day."

He led the way and heard Dennis following him. Lobo would capture any horseman's attention. While Dennis stared in fascination through the small, barred area at the top of the stall door Hearns would have plenty of time to move in and strike.

He stepped back to give Dennis room. He couldn't see Hearns, but he imagined he could hear his tightened breathing. He could visualize how Hearns' hands were sweating as he gripped the club. Damn you, Gig, he thought. Don't you slip up in your timing.

He could prevent that slip-up. He could stand back of Dennis until the man was absorbed in watching Lobo. Then he could move silently to one side. It would leave Hearns a long stride to reach Dennis. Hearns could be as quick as a cat. Dennis shouldn't have enough time even to begin to turn his head.

Dennis peered through the stout bars. Lobo was a blood-red animal with creamy mane and tail. The tail almost brushed the floor, and the mane hung well below his shoulders. Both were tangled and needed currying. A horse this wild would get little personal attention.

The horse was a natural outlaw. Small eyes rolled

in a sea of muddy white, and the nostrils flared each time he snorted. He didn't like human eyes on him—he lunged about the stall throwing his body against the walls. They creaked and groaned under his on-slaughts.

Nobody needed a second glance to see the danger in the horse. This was one of those rare ones that would kill himself with effort before he submitted to man's handling.

Dennis was completely absorbed in watching the animal. Pratt grinned wickedly. He couldn't ask for a setup to be more perfect.

He started to step to one side, and Kate said from the door of the barn, "Orrie! Mr. Dennis! Are you in here?"

Pratt's face twisted with anguish. It would take her only a fraction for her eyes to become accustomed to the shadowy interior. Maybe she had already seen them, for she was moving this way.

Pratt couldn't let Hearns step out and brain Dennis with her watching. He yelled, "Here, Kate," and thought he heard a small, scuffling sound as though Hearns were settling back to his original position.

He moved quickly toward her, and Dennis fol-lowed him. Her eyes were more accustomed to the barn than Dennis' eyes were. She might see Hearns crouching beside the stall.

Her eyes went from one face to the other, and there was worry in them. She said too quickly, "Is any-thing wrong?"

"Why, no," Pratt said hastily. "I was just showing him Lobo before I lined out today's work for him."

"He won't be working for you today." Her voice was crisp. "Will you saddle and ride with me, Mr. Dennis?"

"My pleasure," Dennis murmured, and set to work saddling his and Kate's horses.

Hearns joined Pratt as the echo of the hoofbeats faded away. His face was limp with reaction, and there was a shakiness in his voice.

"My God," he said. "I almost hit him. And with her looking. If I had, do you know what would have happened?"

Pratt's eyes were fixed on him with terrible intensity. "We'd have had to kill her too," Hearns said huskily.

He still carried the broken piece of tongue, and Pratt jerked it from his hand and threw it across the barn. He wanted to call Hearns a damned bungler, but it wouldn't be true. The timing had gone all sour. Usually Kate spent an hour or more cleaning up the kitchen. This morning she had changed into pants and boots and came straight to the barn. He didn't want to admit it, but Hearns was right: if she had seen what Pratt had intended he would have had to kill her to shut her mouth. He was trembling inwardly, and his stomach was churning.

Hearns stared at him in awed fear, and Pratt loosened his pent-up wrath on him.

"Get out of here," he roared. "Get out of here and do some work."

He took a final look in the direction they had taken. Sam Dennis had been a lucky man this morning. That kind of luck couldn't last forever.

VI

Kate and Lee rode a long way in silence. His eyes were busy sweeping the country, and some of the almost forgotten landmarks came back. That bald knob that stood out so prominently to his left—that was familiar.

It was a land of savage contrasts built on immensities of space and ruggedness. The horizontal sweep of the plains was broken by the vertical rise of the mountains. It was good cattle country—when nature was generous. In a good year, three times the ordinary number of cattle a man carried couldn't keep the grass down. But when nature withheld her blessings a man quickly learned that whatever the number of cattle he had was too many.

It must have been a bad winter. While today's sun was comfortably warming, it couldn't wipe out the evidence of a long, hard winter. He saw several bunches of winter-gaunted cows searching out the sparse, new, green growth. They moved listlessly, and it would take several weeks of lush grazing to put strength back into them.

The snow line was retreating sullenly higher up the mountains, and the coulees and streams ran bank full. That was further proof of a hard winter. For it took the melting of a tremendous snow pack to run water like this.

Kate suddenly asked, "Were you in trouble back there in the barn?"

"Why?" Lee's voice was easy.

"I saw the look on Orrie's face. Didn't you see it?"

Lee hadn't missed it. For a moment he had been sure he had seen disappointment mixed with hating blazing out of Pratt's eyes.

"I saw it," he admitted. He didn't say it was quite a change from the Orrie Pratt who had met him at the door.

"What was he doing?"

"Nothing. Just showing me Lobo." He had been fascinated by the raw ferocity of the horse, and Pratt had been standing behind him. Could Kate's presence have prevented something from happening? He shrugged away the ridiculous thought. Pratt wouldn't be foolhardy to try something drastic that close to the house. But just the same, Lee vowed it would be his last careless moment around the man.

He asked, "What will you ever do with Lobo?"

"I don't know," she said dispiritedly. "I don't know how many men have tried to ride him. He hurt a lot of them. I don't know why Cleatis kept him. Unless it was the only thing in his life he couldn't handle."

She went back to the subject that troubled her. "Orrie's changed."

His face was wooden. "How?"

She made a vague gesture. "I'm not really sure. Ever since Newlin was crippled and Cleatis had his first attack——" She broke off and bit her lip. "I don't know exactly how he's changed, except that he seems more positive, more sure of himself. He almost acts as though the Circle A belongs to him. And the way he looks at me——" Her attempt at laughter was a failure. "Isn't that ridiculous?"

It wasn't ridiculous at all. She was an attractive woman, and it wasn't unlikely that Pratt would have ambitions.

"After Cleatis turned the management over to Orrie, all the old men drifted away. I don't like the ones he hired in their place."

Lee didn't comment. But those men *were* a hard-eyed crew. And they took their orders from Pratt; that was plain to see.

He rode for a moment in silence before he said abruptly, "What are you trying to tell me?"

"I don't know," she said helplessly. "I only know that things are getting worse. We're going downhill fast. I don't think we can stand another year of losses like we've had." Her tone picked up a bitter note. "Newlin won't even help with the book work. All he does is sit there thinking about himself."

"What do you want me to do?" he asked harshly. A woman shouldn't be burdened like this. But he didn't want to feel sympathy for her. She was an Ash-baugh, and the name alone made her guilty.

Her eyes searched his face, and something inside of her seemed bursting to be said. But she said flatly, "Our winter kill runs three times as high as anybody else's around us. And we lose stock all through the summer. Orrie says varmints take them."

The summer losses were entirely possible. This was rough country. the natural haunt of bears, lions and wolves. The predators would take their toll. But the percentage of loss shouldn't be high enough to break a ranch.

He said, "Yes," and it was no help.

She took a deep breath. "I want you to find out if our losses are from natural causes or from something else."

"What would that something else be?" he asked softly.

Again she made that helpless little gesture. "I don't know. Management. Something like that."

He wanted to laugh at the irony of it. She was asking him for help—turning to the one person who wanted nothing more than to see the Circle A smashed. Still, it was hard to keep from feeling pity for her. People could be caught in something not of their own making.

His face stiffened as he saw the lightning-blasted stump ahead of them. It had been a huge tree, and the lightning had hit it well up the trunk. But the natural rotting and erosion of the weather had whittled it down until now it was scarcely waist-high. But he remembered it. It lay close to the boundary of the land his father had homesteaded.

She hadn't deviated from the course she had first set. It looked as though she had deliberately brought him here for some reason. It was a ridiculous thought, but struggle as he would he couldn't uproot it. She had been only a child when it had happened, and he doubted that Cleatis had ever talked to her about it. But still she had headed straight here, and he wished he knew why.

He kept an iron control of his face. Only his eyes burned with the savage fire of the old memory. He wanted to turn back. He didn't want to ride onto that land. But he could think of no protest that would seem logical.

They splashed across the stream that ran not a hundred yards from where the house had once stood. The flat rocks on the stream bed must be well moss-covered by now. He remembered how he had struggled helping his father build that ford. Some of those rocks had been murderously heavy.

Each step carried him deeper into some memory, and his breathing came harder. The brush had taken over the cleared land. It took constant effort to keep nature from taking back what man had taken from her.

In his mind's eye he could see the house still standing, and he remembered the pride in his mother's eyes. The firelight lighted that memory, and he could hear the creak and groan of the flame-weakened timbers. He heard his mother's soft crying again and looked at the dispirited muteness of his father.

He shook his head to clear the memory. He breathed hard, and something must surely have shown on his face. He glanced at Kate, but her attention was caught elsewhere.

Then he was in control again, and he looked at the scene dispassionately. The brush had encroached so badly it was hard to pick out the exact site of the cabin. The ashes were all gone, washed away by summer's rains or diluted by winter's snows. He couldn't even find a charred piece of board. Then he remembered how much time had passed. Any remnants of lumber would have rotted and gone back to the earth.

He saw it then. One of the piled-rock foundations was still standing. The other three had fallen and were scattered. He stared at it a long time. It was a pitiful monument to the ending of a man's dreams.

"Will you, Mr. Dennis?"

Her voice brought him out of the trance-like spell. For a moment the ghosts of the past had been real people again crowding in close around him.

Her voice changed all that. Nothing could make those people anything but ghosts.

"Will I what?" he asked roughly.

"Will you help me save the Circle A—" Her pause was only a breath's time. "—Sam," she finished.

He stared sardonically at her. She had called him by his first name. Now she was beginning to use her feminine wiles. She had made a bad mistake in picking this direction to ride. Of course, she couldn't know how seeing this could harden and reset him. And he had been on the verge of feeling pity and sympathy for her.

"Sure I will," he said, and his eyes held a bright, fierce flame. "I'll help you, all right."

He felt no remorse at the lie. He was going to help smash the Circle A. Whatever was happening he'd further it all he could. One day he hoped to see no more left of the ranch than remained of the Martin homestead.

She searched his face, then sighed. He didn't know what the sigh meant, and he didn't care. He was beyond reach of anything she might say or feel.

VII

Before he could further the ruin of the Circle A he had to know what was happening to it now, and he spent days riding the range by himself. He saw much evidence of the winter's kill, and it was heavy. His nose led him to the spots where cattle had died long before they came into view. Rotting carcasses were piled up in canyons or in deep coulees. Snow-blinded, frozen cattle had drifted before a storm until there had been no more earth under their feet. Even if the first few over the canyon's edge had survived the fall the others crashing upon top of them would have killed them.

He sat at the edge of a deep cut in the earth and frowned at the remains of thirty or forty cows. Pratt had made no effort to skin out those carcasses. It would have been a pitiful salvage compared to the live value of the animals, but at least it would have been an attempt to save something.

He counted them as best as he could. Predators had been at those bodies, ripping hide and scattering bones, making it almost impossible to get an exact count. He added this number to the total in his mind. There might be a few more death traps he hadn't discovered, but he thought his estimate of the winter's kill would be reasonably accurate. He'd have to ask Kate what number Pratt had turned in.

He avoided her all he could. Every time he was near her there was some beseeching in her eyes he couldn't answer. He broke off every contact with her with a shake of his head and a muttered, "Nothing."

So far that 'nothing' was the truth. He had watched Pratt and the others ride out; he had watched them at routine tasks. The moment Kate had mentioned excessive losses the thought that someone was rustling them had popped into his mind. Probably not on a big scale, but a steady drain of a dozen to twenty head. Over a period of time losses like that could bleed any ranch white. But if Pratt and the others were involved he had found no proof of it.

He picked his way back from the canyon's edge, letting Amigo find his own way down through the jumble of boulders. His mind was engrossed with too many problems these days, and he sometimes wondered if he was weakening in his original intention. He always cursed just the suggestion of that thought. He wasn't weakening.

The downward path pinched in between two huge boulders, and his right leg scraped against one, jarring him out of his thoughts. He hadn't come up this way. Amigo had picked another path in going back.

The startled woof momentarily froze him and the horse. A full-grown brown bear and two cubs were tearing at a half-devoured calf. He picked up the scene with a sweep of his eyes. The cubs looked like last year's. Sometime later in the season the mother would chase them up a tree, then abandon them to fend for themselves. But now she was defending them, and there wasn't a more dangerous animal alive.

Amigo trembled with fear, and Lee reined him in hard. With his free hand he jerked the rifle from its scabbard. He would have preferred to run, but he had no room. He'd never be able to back Amigo through that narrow passageway between the two rocks just behind him. He could go but one way, and that was forward. And the she-bear blocked it.

Her next woof was much angrier. She cuffed one of the cubs and it scampered for a tree, the other following on its heels. Amigo was dancing and throwing his body around, and Lee couldn't hold him down. The bear was working herself up into a charge. She was close enough for him to see the enraged red of her eyes, and her mouth was wide with its snarling. He had time for one shot, and he'd better make it good.

He aimed between the eyes, hoping to hit the brain pan, and just as he pulled the trigger Amigo lunged. He heard her squeal of rage and pain. He had hit, but he didn't know how well. The shot was the final straw for Amigo; he bolted off the path through the thickest of brush, and Lee couldn't control him. Lee ducked one branch, but the next was too low, and it scraped him out of the saddle.

As he went down, one thought was in his mind. He had to hold onto the rifle.

He hit hard on one shoulder and felt the rocks tear at his flesh. Behind him the squealing was louder. The bear would take time to claw at the stinging hurt he had put in her, but it wouldn't hold her forever.

Blood filled his mouth. He must have bitten his tongue. He was groggy and sick with nausea as he scrambled to his feet. He still held the rifle. Below him he could hear Amigo's crashing path through the brush.

The bear roared at the top of her voice as she came down the mountainside, and for a moment awe held him motionless. He'd never known a bear could cover distance so fast.

He willed the shakiness out of his muscles and the water from his eyes as he snugged the butt to his shoulder. He wouldn't have too many good shots. He pumped a slug into her, but if she slowed that breakneck charge he couldn't see it. He threw another bullet into her, and that one slewed her halfway around. But she recovered and came on again. He had thirty feet between them. She could carry every cartridge in the magazine if none of them were placed in a vital spot.

He forced the panic to retreat and took deliberate time with the third shot. He squeezed the trigger, and she went down as though her legs had been kicked out from under her. She rolled and slid and came to a rest not ten feet from him. He pumped in two more shots before he dared approach her.

Her mouth was open, and the slobber from it ran pink. The evil little eyes were slowly dulling.

Reaction set in, and the shaking took his body. He wiped the back of his hand across his forehead, and it came away wet. He'd never want anything closer.

He rolled a cigarette and grinned bleakly as he noticed the trembling in his hands. His shoulder smarted, and he examined it. He had scraped some skin from it, and it would be bruised and sore by morning. He figured it a small cost for the luck he had had.

The cubs were still up the trees. He aimed at the black balls against the sky for a moment, but then lowered the rifle. He had had enough bear trouble for one day.

He found out how sore and battered he was with the first few steps. But he kept doggedly on, following in the general direction Amigo had taken. Each step increased his fluent swearing at the animal's flight. He hoped the panic hadn't run him clear out of the country.

Lee walked a mile and a half before he found the horse. He was grazing in a small meadow, and he threw up his head at Lee's approach. The horse watched him narrowly, breaking his scrutiny to take little dabs at the grass.

The animal acted as though he were some kind of fearful apparition, and Lee said bitterly, "Damn you, Amigo. If you run some more I swear I'll drop you."

He approached the animal slowly, wheedling him in his softest tones. Amigo shied nervously a few steps and acted as though he were going to bolt.

"Whoa, boy. Steady, boy." He kept up his slow, patient movements, his hand outstretched, his fingers wriggling in invitation.

Amigo's ears went forward and back. Lee wanted to lunge for the reins, but he was too far away. His shoulder throbbed, he was foot-sore, and he ached all over. And on top of all that he had to waste time babying a skittish horse.

He never varied his tone or his approach. He made his final grab quick but smooth. He let out a long sigh as his hand closed on the reins. He rested his arm briefly over the animal's neck.

"You damned hammerhead," he said. "I ought to bust your head. You know that, don't you?"

Amigo whinnied soft agreement.

Lee swung into the saddle, his teeth set against the pain he knew the movement would bring. He turned Amigo toward the house, content to take it slow.

It was suppertime or past before he reached the house. He unsaddled and fed Amigo, then debated upon going in to the kitchen. His light jacket and shirt were torn, and he had some superficial bleeding from the fall. His injuries looked worse than they were.

He shook his head and walked into the kitchen.

They were just pushing back from the table, and heads turned to stare at him. He saw something that might have been terror in Kate's eyes.

Hearns said with heavy humor, "It looks like a bear jumped you."

"One did," Lee said gravely. He recounted the experience briefly, and saw what could have been disappointment in Pratt's face.

"A grizzly?" Hearns asked incredulously.

"A brown. Big enough," Lee said curtly. It might have been a different story if it had been a grizzly. A grizzly was bigger, and it took much more to stop it. He thought of the tiny margin he'd had left with the brown, and took his mind from the unpleasant speculation.

Kate said, "Let me look at that shoulder."

"It's nothing," he protested, but he lost against her insistence.

Her fingers were gentle as she removed his jacket and shirt. She winced as she saw the raw, angry

scrape. She washed it carefully and applied a soothing salve.

Only then did Pratt turn to leave the kitchen. His
eyes were smoky and wicked looking. Before he
stepped outdoors he said loudly, "I told you the
damned varmints were taking our cattle."

He slammed the door angrily behind him.

Lee waited until the others followed Pratt. He kept
his eyes averted from her face. He didn't want to be
grateful to her for anything.

He said gruffly, "How much winter-kill did Pratt
report?"

He didn't look toward the door. He didn't see the
dark shadow beyond it.

She quoted him a figure, and he shook his head.

"Why?" she asked quickly.

"Nothing," he said. It was a much higher figure
than he had tallied. Pratt had lied to cover up missing cattle. Lee was certain he knew who was stealing
Circle A beef. Now the problem was to find out how.

VIII

Pratt walked to the bunkhouse and beckoned Gig
Hearns and Cully Desmonds to follow him outside.

He said, "He's a Cattleman's Association man all
right."

Hearns' eyes were round. Desmonds spit into the dust. He made an elaborate pretense of not being disturbed, but he was. It showed in his tight face.

"How do you know?" Hearns asked.

"I heard him ask her about the winter kill. That's what he's been doing with all his riding around. Tallying the kill. He didn't find as many as I turned in."

Pratt let them digest this, then said, "He knows a lot of cattle are missing. It won't take him long to figure out who's responsible—if he doesn't already know."

He heard the sound of their breathing, and it had a rasping note.

"What are we going to do?" Hearns asked.

"I'm figuring neither of you want to go to jail." Pratt grinned at their angry glances. "Then we'd better stop him before he makes a report."

Their nods were slow and reluctant, but there was agreement in them.

Pratt said, "Follow him around tomorrow until you find the spot you want. Just be sure he doesn't come back."

Desmonds spit again. "They'll send another one."

"We'll worry about that when it happens," Pratt snapped.

They were talking in low voices when he left them. They knew what they had to do. They had no other choice.

Lee awakened late in the morning. He stretched and grimaced. Some beat-up muscles screamed back at him. He worked the shoulder, and, though it was tender, it responded. There wasn't a thing to keep him from riding today. He still had part of his problem to solve. He had to find out how those cattle had been driven out of the valley without anybody being aware of it. It hadn't been by the main road towards town: Kate would have known about it, and too many other eyes would have noticed and speculated.

What are you going to do when you find out? The question formed silently in his mind. He wasn't sure —maybe help Pratt make the final cleanup.

He walked into the kitchen, and Kate had his breakfast ready. His was the only place set at the table. The others were long gone.

He said in a surly voice, "You didn't have to let me sleep. You could've called me."

He could read nothing from her glance.

"I thought you needed the rest." She poured a steaming cup of coffee. She kept her face turned as she asked, "You're not riding again today, are you?"

"Yes," he said harshly. He hoped that would stop her. He didn't want her throwing questions at him.

She let him eat in silence, and he saw the angry set of her chin. He'd trod her toes hard, and it was an effort for her to keep her temper.

He walked to the door and said an ungracious, "Thanks."

He caught the hot flash of her eyes before he stepped outside. For some reason he felt a terrible sense of loss.

He walked to the barn and heard Lobo thrashing about in his stall. He walked to the stall door and peered through the bars. The stall was filthy, and there wasn't any water in the tub. Taking care of the animal could be dangerous, and Lee was sure the horse must know a lot of neglect.

It was wrong to keep an animal penned up like this. Lobo would be better off dead—or free. The idea seized him and wouldn't let go.

He breathed faster as he walked out into the corral adjoining the barn. He shot a surreptitious look at the house, then opened the corral gate. He came back and unlatched the stall door. Then he ran like hell for the barn door and flattened himself against the outside of it. He hoped Lobo would come through the door and see the opened gate. The thought flashed into his mind, *The brute can stop when he gets out into the corral. If he sees you he'll charge you.* If it happened, he decided, he could duck back into the barn. He could maneuver in a much smaller space than Lobo could. He could keep ducking in and out around the barn door until he wore the stallion out.

He heard the sudden thunder of hoofs, and Lobo tore out of the barn. Lee made himself small against the door's surface. Lobo saw that opened gate. Lee breathed freer. Lobo wouldn't stop now. His breath caught as Lobo slammed his hoofs to a sliding stop just as he reached the gate. The horse whipped his body around and faced Lee, his head high. He slashed at the earth, sending dirt sprays behind him.

Lee cursed the animal with all the oaths at his command. He'd had his chance at freedom, and he wasn't taking it. "You Goddamned idiot," he said. He didn't dare yell at the animal. "The gate's open behind you."

The horse quieted. He stood there a long moment looking at Lee. Lee was poised on his toes, ready to move in a hurry. Even as he waited tensely for the animal's next move, a thrill of appreciation ran through him. He was a magnificent animal. The sun struck burnished rays from his coat and bathed the powerful chest and long, clean legs. It was too bad the horse couldn't be adapted for man's use.

It seemed a long time that they stood rooted looking at each other. Then Lobo suddenly whirled and tore out of the gate at full run. His mane and tail streamed out behind him, and Lee watched in open-mouthed awe until he was out of sight. That horse didn't run—he flew.

He felt no regret at his action, though he did cast a guilty look at the house. He could see only one of two ends for the animal—freedom or a bullet in the head. It was better to turn him loose.

He saw no one peering at him from a window. He had gone ahead without asking permission, and somebody might raise hell about it. He went back into the barn and looked about for a tool of some kind. That broken piece of wagon tongue would do just fine, and he picked it up.

He battered the latch until it was barely hanging. He splintered a couple of boards on the inside of the stall. Then examined his work judiciously. Who could prove that Lobo hadn't kicked the latch loose?

He grinned, and went to saddle Amigo. When he returned this evening he would be as surprised as anybody to hear that Lobo had broken loose. And if somebody proposed a party to recapture the animal Lee wasn't going to be crazy enough to be a part of it.

He rode out in the general direction Lobo had taken. He rode slowly, trying not to miss a single detail. The stubborn thought persisted in his mind that there had to be another way through the mountains, a passage through which cattle could be moved. But wouldn't Kate know about it? He frowned at the thought. Not necessarily. This was big country, and a person might search for some such passage without ever finding it. It might not exist, either, he concluded. But he wouldn't give that thought much harbor until he was thoroughly convinced.

By mid-afternoon the enormity of his search was beginning to hit him. He looked at the towering mountains and the rough foothill country and shook his head slowly.

He swore at himself for the depression. He was a damned fool if he expected to find it in a day's searching.

He found a half-dozen possible leads, and each petered out against some rocky bulwark. Then he had to turn and retrace his steps. He squinted at the sun. He guessed he'd about had it for the day. It would almost be dark now before he got back.

He heard the wild trumpeting of a stallion's voice.

It contained challenge and joy. He swung his head around to locate the horse, and got just a glimpse of it. It stood on the rimrock, outlined against the sky, its coat looking redder than ever in the fading sun.

Jerking his head around to locate the stallion saved his life. He didn't hear the report of the rifle, but he heard the nasty whine of the bullet, and the breath of its passage burned his cheek.

IX

Some instinct moved him, and he half fell, half dived from the saddle. The moment he hit the ground he knew he had made a grave mistake. He should have stayed in the saddle and run for it.

That conclusion was followed by another shot, and it changed his mind. That shot came from high ground and on the opposite side from the first. It was a good two hundred yards to cover of any kind, and they had him bracketed. It would be a relatively easy matter for a marksman to pick him out of the saddle. He lay listening to the fading echoes of Amigo's hoofs, and suddenly this was the loneliest spot he had ever known in his life.

Another shot geysered dirt over him. He lay limply against the ground, his teeth locked in anticipation of a bullet thudding into his flesh. He was committed now. All he could do was lay here and pray they wouldn't shoot again. Surely they wouldn't waste more shells on what appeared to be a dead man.

He was bathed in his own sweat as he waited, and each minute was an eternity long. After eons had passed, he dared to hope that his deception might be successful. But he didn't make the mistake of stirring.

He heard the chattering of a whisky jay, and out of the corner of his eye he saw the bird light on the ground. It hopped several steps toward him, then retreated. Finally, emboldened by its curiosity, it came quite near, and he saw the bright beady eyes cocked first one way, then the other.

He made his breathing shallow and slow. The bird came closer, and he lost sight of it. Then he felt its weight on his outflung arm. A man can live a long time without breathing. He proved it. If the bird took alarm and flew off in squawking flight he was a dead man.

The bird hopped to his wrist and pecked at the button on the cuff of his jacket.

He was still under scrutiny; he could feel it as though it was a physical force. He wanted to scream at the unseen watchers. What more proof did they want than the actions of the jay?

His right arm was under his body, and his muscles began to ache. He didn't know how much longer he could hold this position without moving.

His heart lodged in his throat as the bird flew off in screaming alarm. He didn't see how, but he must have given himself away to frighten it like that. His jaws hurt from the pressure he put on them, and he wanted to cry out against the bullet he knew was coming.

Then he heard the slow, walking beat of horses' hoofs coming toward him. He let out a shallow breath. Those horses had been the cause of the bird's flight.

They were near enough for him to hear a voice say, "Think I should put another shot in him?"

"What for?" a second voice answered. "Unless you want to waste a shell. You saw how that jay acted."

The hoof sound didn't stop, and Lee breathed again. Evidently, the first voice was satisfied. He sucked in his stomach, giving his pinioned hand a little room, and inched it toward his holstered gun. His hand closed on the butt, and he drew it out a fraction of an inch at a time.

He could see a horse's legs now; then Gig Hearns said, "This worked out real well. I thought we'd lost him. Wouldn't Orrie have raised hell if we had?"

"We couldn't have picked a better spot," Desmonds said. "And he rode right into it."

"Let's see if he's got anything on him," Hearns said.

Lee waited until he heard the creaking of saddle leather before he rolled and came to a sitting position. Hearns was on the ground, but Desmonds still had one foot in the stirrup.

They saw the gun in his hand, and their faces went slack with surprised fear. Hearns said, "Oh my God."

Lee shot him in the head, and Hearns' fear was blotted out by a sweeping flow of blood. He went over backwards, and Lee spun to get a better aim at

Desmonds. The man's foot was still in the stirrup, and he was caught in indecision—to step to the ground or swing back into the saddle.

His horse went wild at the shot and danced around in a half circle, pulling Desmonds off balance. He cursed it and tried to jerk it to him. He must have decided to swing up, for his foot left the ground.

Lee shot him on the rise, hitting him before the leg was across the saddle. He heard Desmonds' harsh grunt, and fired again. Both shots were solid body hits, and the second wiped all life away. Desmonds fell limply toward the ground, his body twisting at an awkward angle. His fall, and the horse's sudden lunge, trapped his foot in the stirrup. The horse bolted, trailing a dangling, bouncing weight behind it.

Lee stood, and his legs didn't want to support him. He breathed in great gulps, and his air-starved lungs slowly eased.

He rolled and smoked a cigarette before the shakiness left him. He had stared into death's face, and it was always an ugly one.

He looked up at the rimrock where the stallion had stood outlined against the sky. The horse was gone.

He said softly, "Lobo, you don't owe me a thing."

He gazed at Hearns' body, a cold anger in his eyes. Nothing was as deadly or as dirty as a bushwhacker. But Hearns and Desmonds had been only the tools. Lee wanted the hand that had used them. He thought of jumping Pratt the moment he got back. His accusation would stamp guilt on Pratt's face, and he would need no other reason to kill him. He let the thought slip away. It might be more satisfying to see Pratt's nerves grow tighter and tighter—and they would, when the two men he had sent out didn't return.

Hearns' horse had bolted in the opposite direction from the way Desmonds' horse had taken. Lee was afoot again. He decided to take out after Desmonds' mount. Even with panic driving it, that dragging weight from the stirrup would wear the horse down pretty quick. Once he had rounded up Desmonds' horse it would be no trick to collect Hearns' mount and Amigo. If he abandoned his original intention to load the bodies on their horses and take them back to the ranch, what would he do with them? He nodded slowly. Bury them and watch Pratt's nerves fray as he searched for them.

He was right about the awkward weight wearing down Desmonds' horse. He caught up with it in less than a half mile. The horse kept shying from him. It took a lot of patience and more soothing words to quiet it enough for Lee to grab the reins.

Desmonds wasn't a pretty sight. Dragging him over the rough terrain had torn him up considerably, and the horse had added additional damage by kicking the body, trying to dislodge it. Desmonds had been lucky to be dead before his horse had bolted.

Lee had to tie the horse to a tree before he could free Desmonds' feet. He needed both hands, and even then it was a hard job. The leg was broken, and the inanimate weight of the body made it difficult to handle. He had to lift and turn it at the same time. He was sweating and cursing by the time the foot finally slid out of the stirrup.

He laid Desmonds across the saddle and led the horse back to where Hearns lay. He tugged on the body, and it fell sprawling grotesquely on the ground. Now he had to catch Hearns' horse and Amigo.

He found them and brought them back without too much trouble. He looked around at the rocky ground. Burying the two men was going to be a hard job, if not impossible. He didn't have a tool of any kind, and with a stick he could do little more than scrape the shallowest of depressions. And what was he going to do with their horses?

Both of the animals were mares, and his eyes gleamed as he looked at them. He stripped saddles and bridles off of them, and he laughed as he whacked them on the rumps. He was still grinning as he watched them gallop away. They were heading up into the mountains, and he hoped they wouldn't turn later on and return to the ranch. He hoped Lobo would find them first. Lobo needed a start for his harem.

He dragged the bodies to a narrow, deep crevice in the rock. He shoved them over, and he didn't wince as he heard them hit. He carried the saddles and gear to the crevice and threw them in on top of the bodies. He looked around for the first rock to roll into the crevice. They were plentifully scattered along here.

All he had to do was bring them to this spot for the final push.

He worked the better part of two hours. Some of the rocks were too big to be carried, and he rolled them along the ground. When he had finished, the ache in his back told him how many rocks he had carried.

He looked into the crevice. The rocks were piled high. Even the most determined predator couldn't get at Hearns and Desmonds now, though that wasn't his chief consideration. He didn't want man to find them either.

He stared into the crevice for quite awhile. Not a sign of anything human showed. Pratt and the others could search their damned heads off, and they'd never find the missing men.

He walked to Amigo and swung into the saddle. This mystery would drive Pratt crazy. He would look at Lee and wonder, but he wouldn't be able to put into words the questions in his mind that were driving him crazy. They would be like sharp teeth gnawing him to pieces from the inside.

Lee turned Amigo toward the ranch house. His face was sober. It had been a rough afternoon.

X

He had been right about the unasked questions driving Pratt crazy. A dozen times Lee was sure Pratt was going to blurt them out. The man would stare at Lee, and his mouth would partially open. Then he'd snap it shut, and his eyes would grow more wild.

Pratt looked for Hearns and Desmonds. He kept his men in the saddle from morning to night for five days. And each evening when he returned his eyes were more baffled.

Kate tried to talk to Lee about it, and he gave her a few unsatisfactory words in return or nothing at all.

"They simply couldn't have just vanished," she said angrily.

"Maybe they got tired of this place and rode off."

"They had pay coming to them," she said scornfully. "And all their personal things in the bunkhouse."

His shrug further angered her. "You're not even looking for them," she cried.

"I'm looking," he said. He was, but not for Hearns and Desmonds. He was scouring the land looking for a break in the mountains, a break that would let cattle be driven through with the minimum of people knowing about it. His conviction was beginning to weaken. Maybe the winter kill and the varmints had taken the toll Pratt said they had.

He walked away to saddle Amigo. After he mounted, he looked back. She was still there, and he lifted his arm. She didn't respond. It suited him fine. He'd rather have anger between them. It would make any future decision and action a lot easier.

Kate watched Lee until he was out of sight. Pratt came out of the bunkhouse and approached her. Some inward devils were making his face haggard.

At the question in her eyes he said sullenly, "I didn't feel up to riding today. I sent the others out." It didn't lessen the accusation in her eyes, and he said angrily, "You tell me where to look. They just vanished."

"I think you'd better get Homer out here," she said quietly.

"No," he almost yelled. His vehemence put a startled look in her eyes. He said lamely, "We've always handled what we had to without calling in the law." He didn't want Homer Iman poking and prying around out here.

Her eyes held a warning she didn't voice before she turned and walked into the house. She would give him only a little more time before she took direct responsibility.

He walked back to the bunkhouse and threw himself on his bunk. He lay there a few seconds before he got to his feet. His tortured thoughts wouldn't let him lie still. He was positive that Dennis had something to do with this. But how was he going to find out?

He strode the length of the bunkhouse, then retraced his steps, his hands balled. What had happened out there? Where were Hearns and Desmonds?

He opened his war bag and pulled out a bottle. It infuriated Kate to have him drink around here. He snarled at the thought of her. Right now he didn't care what she thought. He needed it.

He sat down and upended the bottle. The whisky hammered along his bloodstream, warming him. It couldn't do a thing to dull his thoughts. He knew he had to do something before panic stampeded him into some foolish action. It had all started with Dennis' arrival here. He should have killed him the moment he'd seen him here. But no—he had turned clever, trying to build up a logical excuse. Well, he didn't need an excuse anymore. He'd shoot him when he rode in. He was positive that Dennis had killed Hearns and Desmonds. That was all the excuse he needed.

The bottle was half empty when he heard the slam of hoofs. Anger blackened his face. If his men were coming in before the day was done he'd take hide off of them. Then rational thought took over. He heard only one horse. It couldn't be his men.

His face was raw with violence as he thought that it could be Dennis coming back for some reason. If it was, here was the opportunity he was looking for.

He grabbed a rifle from its rack of horns and moved to a window facing the house. The whisky had enflamed him beyond any power of reason to stop him.

He peeked out of the window and cursed bitterly.

Homer Iman was just swinging down to the ground, and the fact that it wasn't Dennis seemed to Pratt a lost opportunity at the moment.

Reason returned, pushing back the whisky's hold. As the thoughts formed clearly in his head they built an anger. So Kate had gone against his warning; she had sent for Iman despite what he had told her.

At the height of his anger against her it suddenly burst like an overstrained balloon. "I'm not thinking good," he muttered. There hadn't been enough time for her to send somebody to Iman and for him to get back. Besides, who could she have sent? He knew where everybody was but Dennis. His eyes narrowed in concentration. Had she sent Dennis after Iman early this morning—before she'd even spoken to him?

"Yes," he said savagely. "That's what she's done." Dennis hadn't ridden back with Iman. That was to deceive him into believing they weren't working again. If Dennis was real smart he'd never come back.

Pratt pulled at his fingers. He wished he knew what Kate and Iman were talking about. His face brightened. If she took Iman into the parlor he might be able to slip up to the front window and listen. It was worth the risk. What could happen beyond Kate bawling him out if she saw him?

He put the rifle back in place and moved toward the house. He didn't hear any sound coming from the kitchen as he passed it. Kate must have asked Iman into the parlor. He edged to the front of the house, then stepped hastily back, a soft curse in his throat.

On nice days Newlin often sat out on the front porch. He was out here now, his head drooping as he dozed.

Pratt knew a stab of rage at him. Newlin blocked him from using the front window. He'd never had much worth even when his legs had been good. He'd knuckled under to Cleatis on every count. Not once had Pratt seen Newlin stand up to his father. He'd been no good then, and he was sure worthless now. When an animal had lost its worth it was shot. It was too bad people weren't handled the same way.

He'd have to try the window on the east side of the house, and he pulled back and retraced his steps. He went around the back of the house, then sidled along the side of it. He could hear voices before he reached the window, and he nodded in satisfaction. That window was about half open.

He pressed against the side of it, and most of the words drifted to him clear and distinct. Only now and then was a word garbled.

Kate said, "All right, Homer. You've beat around the bush long enough. You've said everything but what's on your mind."

Iman said evasively, "Kate, I don't know what you're talking about. I ride out for a sociable call. and you jump all over me."

Kate laughed. "Homer, the one thing you aren't is a liar. It's been two years since you've paid us a social call. Now what did you come out here for?"

Iman cleared his throat. "Maybe I'm poking my nose into business that doesn't belong to me."

He was silent a moment, and Kate said, "Go on."

"I just heard you hired a new hand. A Sam something or other."

"Do you mean Sam Dennis?"

"So that's what he's calling himself," Iman growled. "He's got a familiar look about him, but I can't place him. I've gone through a million old Wanted posters. I cant find him. But I know his kind —he's on record somewhere."

Pratt blinked his eyes in surprise. Dennis wasn't an Association man at all, or Iman would know it. Then who was he, and what was he here for?

Iman was talking again, and Pratt put his attention on Iman's words.

Iman said earnestly, "Kate, you can't just hire anybody that wanders in here. A man like Sam Dennis could do you a lot of harm. Sam Dennis." He snorted. "I'll bet that isn't even his real name."

She laughed again. "You'd win your bet. It isn't."

Pratt expected an explosion. Iman was an impatient man when he thought somebody was trying to hide something from him.

But Iman said in an ominously calm voice, "I think now you'd better talk a little, Kate."

Kate said, "Don't get your temper up, Homer. He's Lee Martin."

"Lee Martin," Iman muttered. "Lee Martin."

From the tone of Iman's voice Pratt knew he was trying to place the name. He was doing the same thing himself.

"We've got a better reason to remember him than you have, Homer. He was pretty young the last time you saw him. You see, the Ashbaughs burned out his family."

"Harvey Martin," Iman snorted. "The home-steader. I knew his house burned. But he didn't make any complaint. I just thought he lost heart and rode off. Are you sure?"

"We did it, Homer. Newlin told me after he was hurt. When a person has nothing to do but sit, things prey on his mind. He said Cleatis made him go along. I believe him."

Iman still wasn't convinced. "Maybe somebody's preying on your mind too, Kate. It happened a long time ago. Did he tell you he was Lee Martin?"

"No," she admitted. "But I know. I recognized him at Cleatis' funeral. And the first day after he came here we rode across the old Martin homestead. I saw his face."

The silence was so long that Pratt thought they must have left the room. He was almost tempted to peek through the window and see.

Then Iman said, "I wouldn't remember a kid too well. I got enough faces in my head without trying to pack in kids' faces. But that's why he looked fa-miliar. What did he come back for?"

"I don't know."

"Does he know who burned them out?"

"Newlin said Lee saw them all there."

"Then you know why he came back," Iman said grimly. "I understand a lot of things now."

"What do you understand, Homer?" she asked quietly.

"I don't know why it took him so long to come back, but he's here to get even. I saw his face when he looked at Orrie. I saw it again when he talked to Cleatis. He came back for revenge."

"Do you think he'd make war on a woman and a cripple?"

"Yes," Iman said bluntly. "When a man carries a hate as long as he has it twists him. You're out of your head if you let him stay around another day."

"Do you think sending him away would change him, Homer?"

Iman swore softly. "Kate, if you've got some crazy kind of a thought that by being kind to him you'll change the way he feels, you're——" He broke off helplessly.

Pratt nodded slowly. He knew what Iman was up against. Kate must have that stubborn look on her face. Pratt knew it well. Iman was helpless against it.

"All right, Kate," Iman said heavily. "You won't send him away. Then I'll wait right here until he gets back. I'll straighten him out. I'll put a warning to him that even he can understand."

"No," she said sharply. "I want you to leave him alone. I mean it, Homer. He hasn't done anything. He hadn't done anything before, and we ran him out. Now you want to do the same thing again."

Iman said another soft oath. "It's your land, and you run things here. But I think you're crazy. You can get Orrie or Newlin killed. Do you want that responsibility? It's going to be yours. You remember that. I won't jump him now. But I'm going to keep an eye on him. And the first thing that happens I'm yanking him in. You keep that in mind too."

"I will, Homer." Her voice was strained. "Don't you think I've thought of all that? But don't you see we owe him something?"

Pratt thought it was time to move away. He had heard a chair squeak as though weight was being removed from it. Iman or Kate must have stood.

He slipped along the side of the house to the rear, then crossed hurriedly to the bunkhouse. He found his bottle again and took a long pull. He was surprised to find a little shaking in his hands. Lee Martin! He didn't remember the name or the face. He plodded back through the dark corridors of the past to the night of the fire. If he remembered right, there had been a couple of kids there. But he couldn't recall any details. This Martin's hate had to be solely against the Ashbaughs. He had to know that anything Orrie Pratt had done was under Cleatis' orders.

He cursed the shakiness in his hands and took another drink. This Martin was fast with his hands and too good with a gun. He had ample evidence of both. But if Martin had come here after him, wouldn't something have happened before now?

He built up a favorable answer to the question and drew assurance from it. Sure it would have. Martin was only after the Ashbaughs. *The fight in the saloon was my fault*, Pratt thought. *I got in his way, and he belted me one. That's all it meant.*

He held out his hand. The shakiness was gone. He had nothing to fear from Lee Martin. In a way, him being here could work out for the best. Iman knew of Martin's hatred for the Ashbaughs. If anything happened Iman would jump to the automatic conclusion that Martin was involved.

Pratt's eyes gleamed as he set the bottle down. He didn't need any more of its help. He wasn't too worried about Hearns and Desmonds any more. Maybe Martin had killed them, but if he had, it had to be because he had discovered their ambush. He wouldn't know that Pratt had set them on him.

Each thought built more confidence in him. He walked to the window and watched Iman ride away. Iman had warned Kate he was going to keep an eye on Martin, and for a moment the thought was disturbing. Would Iman learn of what Pratt was doing?

He shrugged away the alarm. Iman would be too engrossed watching Martin. And besides, it was a long way from town out here. Iman couldn't spend too much time out here.

Why hadn't she said something to Iman about Hearns and Desmonds? Pratt's face darkened at the obvious answer. Was she afraid Iman would blame Martin for it? Was she soft on this Lee Martin?

He pushed aside the ridiculous conclusion. How could she be soft on him? She'd known him for only a short while when she was a kid, and he hadn't been back long enough to change anything. No, it had to be the pity in her. She felt the Ashbaughs had done him a terrible wrong, and she was trying to make some kind of repayment.

He threw back his head and laughed. All his worrying had been for nothing. He could go ahead and strip the Circle A; he could steal every head on it, then a bullet in the back would take care of Martin. Iman was already suspicious of him. He would accept any explanation Orrie Pratt gave him.

He stared at the house a long time, and his wanting for her burned him. He wouldn't have to suppress that wanting much longer. After he broke the Circle A, who else would she be able to turn to?

XI

Lee noticed the change in Pratt the following morning. Pratt didn't jerk his eyes away as quickly when Lee looked at him, and there was no fear in them. Instead, he was quite sure a taunting mockery had replaced the shadows he had seen in Pratt's eyes the past few days.

Lee thought, *He acts like he's learned something that's important to him.* Would the discovery of Hearns' and Desmonds' bodies make that difference? Lee gave it some consideration, then dismissed it. If Pratt had found them it would have put something in his face, an anger or a frustration, but not this gloating.

He felt a prickling along his skin. Some instinct was awakening and trying to warn him about something. He thought irritably, *Nothing's changed. He'll try to kill me any chance he gets. I've known that for some time.*

He glanced at Kate, and her eyes were downcast. He had noticed an awful change in her since he'd arrived here. Her cheeks seemed to have hollowed, and the radiance in her eyes was missing. Come to think of it, he hadn't heard her laugh in days. He appraised her soberly. He guessed she didn't have anything to laugh about. He glanced at Newlin with savage criticism. Sure the man was crippled, but he wasn't helping himself or anybody else by his attitude. He wore his self-pity like a new coat, and he wanted everybody to see it.

Damn it, Lee growled to himself, *he could at least be cheerful. It'd help her that much.*

"Newlin," Kate said quietly. "You're not eating."

"I'm not hungry," he answered in a surly tone.

Lee marveled at her patience. She had to wheedle him into eating every bite. If she let him go hungry for a few days, that would change in a hurry.

His appetite was suddenly gone, and he pushed back his chair and stood. Kate looked at his unfinished breakfast and raised her eyes questioningly to him.

He shook his head and walked to the door. Pratt and Kate were both watching him. The mockery was in Pratt's eyes again; Kate's eyes just looked plain worried.

He closed the door violently. All right, he knew she was carrying too much of a load, but was it his fault?

He was in an angry mood as he saddled Amigo. What was he really doing here anyway? He was fighting a woman and a cripple, and he wasn't getting nearly the satisfaction he should out of it. Orrie Pratt was here too, he reminded himself. But Pratt hadn't been the instigator of the burning, and Lee doubted that Newlin had had a dominant say in it either. No, the chief instigator was dead, and it left him only shadows to fight.

He said furiously, "You're getting soft-minded. Finish what you came here to do. Then get out of here."

He mounted and put Amigo in motion. He had covered the south end of the valley pretty thoroughly, so he headed in the opposite direction. A great number of the cattle seemed to have drifted toward the upper end of the valley, and he cast a critical look at them. The grass was stronger, and it seemed to have given them more strength. Many of the cows had new calves following them, and it was lucky they hadn't been born during the last thrust of winter. A cow couldn't get a new-born calf dry and up off the snow in time to keep the cold from claiming it.

His eyes burned as he saw the huge circle as big as a dinner plate with its big A in the center. One of these days that brand wouldn't be in existence. That was the only thing he had to keep in mind.

He had covered a lot of ground by noon, and he hadn't turned up a thing. He had followed a dozen canyons that had seemed as though they could be natural passages through the mountains, and each had ended against a blind wall.

He shook his head in angry frustration. He had been so damned sure that he'd had it all worked out neatly in his head—that Orrie Pratt and the men he had hired were the rustlers. If they were, they had to have a way to get the cattle out of the valley—and there was no such way.

He turned into the mouth of a new canyon, and after a mile it started climbing on him. He looked at the towering mass of the mountain chain ahead of him and shook his head. This wouldn't be it either. The canyon became steeper and more difficult to negotiate. A man would be a damned fool to try to drive cattle this way. They would fight the incline every step of the way, and if they ever stampeded back toward the valley the riders driving them had better pray. There would be nothing else left to them.

The canyon shelved abruptly against a sheer face, and Amigo had difficulty scrambling the last few steps. Lee let him blow on a little flat shelf, and looked around him. He hated to return down that tough climb. He saw a game trail leading to his right, a narrow path suspended against the rock face. Here it was wide enough for a horse to take, but it could peter out around the next bend. He took it, thinking he could always stop and retrace his steps. Though the hope was small, this trail could lead to an easier descent.

He came out on a high promontory, and the valley lay spread out before him. He swore in disgust. A deer or a mountain goat might find its way down from here; he and Amigo couldn't.

He dismounted and rolled a cigarette. He had a long torturous trip back, and he was reluctant to begin it. He said ruefully, "Amigo, I led us into something this time."

Amigo bobbed his head and snorted, and Lee grinned.

"You don't have to agree so hard."

His eyes swept the valley. Had had climbed higher than he'd realized. Cattle on the valley floor looked like small dots. He frowned at the dust being raised down there. Those dots were moving fast, and cattle rarely moved this fast unless they were disturbed.

He pulled a pair of field glasses from his saddle bags and adjusted them. Riders and cattle were amplified in size, and those riders were chousing cattle ahead of them. He saw two riders bring a dozen head out of a brushy draw, turn them toward the ever-growing mass of the herd, then disappear for more.

The glasses magnified the riders well enough for him to recognize them. He saw Pratt's waving arm as he gave directions, and watched him for awhile. He lowered the glasses and frowned. He had heard nothing about a roundup, and this one was being held early, too early to take care of the spring branding and castrating. A lot of the calves hadn't come yet. Pratt should know that by holding his roundup this early he was only going to have to redo work. Unless —Lee sucked in his breath and put the glasses back to his eyes.

Some of the cows were being cut back, and Lee would bet those were the ones heavy with calf. All the steers and the two-year old heifers or better were being included in the hold herd. This was the beef that meant this year's revenue to the ranch. Its loss could be a crippling blow. Lee's face was blank as he watched the growing numbers. Here it was all laid out before him. He could join Pratt and help him, and the Circle A would go under. But what about Pratt? The thought hammered at him, and he gave it an indefinite answer. He could take care of Pratt later.

He put away the glasses and took Amigo's reins. He would have to lead him back down the steepest descent. He wanted to talk to Kate and confirm what he suspected. He still didn't know how the cattle were driven out of the valley. But the passage should be close to where the gather was being made. Pratt would want to make his drive as short as he could.

It was almost dark when he walked into the kitchen. The table had only three places laid.

He asked casually, "Won't Pratt and the others be in?"

Kate shook her head. "No. He's getting ready for the spring branding. He set up camp in the upper end of the valley. He wants to get an early start in the morning."

He had never seen her eyes so infinitely weary, and there were tension lines around her mouth.

He said, "What is it, Kate?" and there was no harshness in his voice.

She tried to smile, and it was a flat failure. "I went in to the bank today. Mr. Jamison is unhappy about my note. We haven't paid too much on it lately. He finally promised to wait until fall. If we have a good shipment we can just squeak by."

He switched his eyes, afraid of what she might see in them. She wouldn't have any shipment at all. Pratt and his busy men would see to that. And Lee didn't have to participate in any way. Here it was all wrapped up neatly and handed to him. He could ride away and forget the Circle A, and next year the bank would own it. He should feel a sweeping tide of satisfaction, and all he felt was a sour flatness. He didn't even have to kill Pratt. All he had to do was tell Iman, and the law would finish the job for him.

Her eyes had a beseeching intensity. "There *will* be a fall shipment, won't there?"

She was begging for help, and he couldn't extend even a finger to her.

"How do I know?" he asked irritably, and walked out of the kitchen.

XII

In the morning, thick, ominous-looking clouds were gathering over the mountains. Already the higher peaks were obscured. Lee studied those clouds, then went back and got his slicker. Wind was tearing at those clouds, ripping off tattered shreds of gray, filmy gauze. The fat bellies of those clouds were moisture-laden, and when they grew heavy enough they would sage into the valley. Snow would fall in the higher elevations, and the valley would receive rain. He shook his head. The country didn't need noisture right now. But man's needs and nature's whims rarely coincided. Nature could be as infuriating as a capricious woman, giving too much or too little. Later on, in the summer, ranchers would pray for just the sight of fat, moisture-bulged clouds—and only the brassy sun would mock them. He shook his head again. He guessed man's quarrel with weather would never be ended.

Animals had an instinct for a coming storm. Amigo didn't want to leave the shelter of the barn. He snorted and dug in his hoofs, and Lee had to drag him outside.

He said impatiently, "I'm not any happier about it than you are."

He looked at the house before he rode off. He wouldn't be seeing it much longer. His plan was full-born and laid out before him. All he needed to put the finishing touches on it was to find out how Pratt got the cattle out of the valley. Then he'd let Iman step in and take over. The Circle A would be broke, and Pratt would serve a long stretch in the pen. There would be no violence, and he wouldn't be pulled into it in any way. It should all be highly satisfactory, yet instead he had a sour taste in his mouth.

He turned north, and a few drops pattered down

into his face. A spring rain could be warm or cold. This one was cold, and he saw Amigo's hide witch under its touch. He thought sardonically, *Pratt must be cursing this storm. It'll delay his drive.*

He reached for his slicker, then didn't untie it. Those first few drops had been only a warning. The storm was holding off for a little longer.

He didn't want to be seen by Pratt and the others, so he kept to the rough country at the valley's edge. He still believed stubbornly that Pratt would gather his herd near the passage out of the valley.

He thought sourly, *You'll look like a damn fool if Pratt is only going about the ranch's business, if there's no passage.* But he wouldn't accept that. Pratt was gathering the best beef on the ranch for some purpose.

He kept up his slow, dogged search. It had to be well-hidden, or Kate would have known about it. He couldn't keep her out of his mind. He remembered how her eyes had lighted the first afternoon he had come here. It had been a long time since he had seen that radiance. She had expected something from him he couldn't give. He shifted against the saddle's hard surface. It was her misfortune she had picked the wrong man.

The rain started in earnest shortly before noon. Something ripped the bellies of those clouds, and the water came down in long, slanting sheets. Amigo kept turning his head against the force of the rain, and it gathered on Lee's hat brim and trickled down the neck of his slicker.

He said, "All right, Amigo. I guess you're smarter than I am." Anyway, it was useless trying to see anything in this weather. The pelting rain and the low-hanging clouds limited his vision until seeing was only a matter of yards.

He looked for a cave or an overhang, anything that would give some kind of shelter. He turned into the mouth of a canyon, and he thought this one would be like all the others he had checked out. It would run for awhile before it lost its width, then peter out against the rock's features. But he might find his cave or an overhanging ledge in it that would offer him protection from the worst of the rain.

He traveled it some five hundred yards, and he was right about it. It petered out in a box end. He cursed at the blank wall and turned back within twenty yards of it. He could see that far. There was no need to ride clear to it.

He stopped Amigo beneath a tiny overhang and slashed the water from his face with his fingers. This protection wasn't much, but he could spend hours riding in this storm and not find better. By pressing tightly against the rock he could keep some of the rain off of him.

He cursed the weather. Sometimes these mountain storms sprang up quickly and viciously and passed almost as soon as they had come. And again they could hold for hours.

He said, "Amigo, if it holds we've got a long, wet ride back."

He reached under his slicker and dired his hands on his pants. He rolled a cigarette and managed to light it with the third match. His fingers were still wet enough to dampen the paper, but by drawing hard he got enough fire to dry the cigarette's dampness.

A frown set his face as he smoked. He could hear the rush of water from someplace, and he saw the dark streaks of it sliding down the canyon walls. A canyon like this acted like a funnel, and all the water that fell within a large surrounding area rushed into it. What had been a dry bed a half-hour before could become a raging torrent. He would have to keep an eye on the canyon floor. If that water started rising he would have to hustle Amigo out of here in a hurry.

The frown remained on his face. Water kept streaking down the canyon walls, but he could see no appreciable change in the level on the floor. That water had to go someplace, and this rocky soil would absorb very little of it. He thought he could hear the rush and gurgle of water. He knew how deceptive the eye was. What appeared to be level could definitely slant either way. The canyon floor wasn't slanting this way, for no water ran past him. And if it slanted the other way, why wasn't the water rising against the wall of the box end?

It had to have some outlet there. That could be the only possible answer.

His eyes kept sweeping back and forth across the canyon floor. That flat, round rock looked out of place against the bigger, jagged ones. And a dozen feet beyond it was another. Erosion could wear rocks into strange shapes, but neither of these looked natural.

He cursed himself for a fool. As familiar as he was with cattle droppings, his mind had been so occupied with other things that he hadn't seen those two pieces of dung at all.

He walked out to the first one and turned the pancake-shaped object over with a boot toe. This manure had been dropped quite a while ago, for it was dried brittle—though the rain was beginning to soften it. He walked to the second one, and he could see a third one twenty feet closer to the wall.

Mounting excitement ran through him. There was no grass in this canyon to pull cattle in here, and three piles of manure so closely spaced said it was likely more than one head had been in here. Of course a cow brute could wander anywhere, but this rocky cut would be the most unlikely place Lee would pick to look for one. Unless they had been driven in here—

His eyes gleamed. If they had been driven in here there had to be a reason.

He walked back to the overhang and tied Amigo's reins to a large rock. Then he turned and walked toward the box end.

He was almost against it before he saw the dark slash that cut off from the blankness at an abrupt angle. A man could pass close to it and think the opening was no more than another shadow on the canyon wall.

It was a narrow opening, barricaded by poles and brush wired together. He removed the barricade and stepped through. No more than two head of cattle could pass through it at once.

Water rushed around his boots. The flooring here was definitely lower than behind him. The water came well up on his boots, and it wouldn't take much distance for it to soak through the leather. He walked along the narrow crevice, feeling oppressed by the close bleakness of the towering walls. He kept an eye on the water, ready to beat a hasty retreat if it seemed to be rising. It could very easily trap a man here.

The cut widened after a hundred yards, and he walked a long way into it. He thought once of going back and getting Amigo, but the excitement of his discovery wouldn't let him waste that much time.

He found other droppings, old ones. Cattle had been driven through here sometime in the past. It would be hell getting them through that narrow opening, but hard-pushing riders in the rear could force cattle into it. Orrie Pratt had driven cattle through here before, and he intended driving more through it very soon.

The floor of the cut hadn't climbed a foot when Lee turned back. Without going to its end he knew it ran straight through the mountains, a natural pass made in some distant time by the savage upheaval and tilting of the earth. It would come out somewhere on the other side, and Pratt had accomplished the most dangerous part of his stealing—that of moving the cattle out of the valley without being seen.

Lee's feet were thoroughly soaked when he turned back. Maybe Cleatis had known about it and dismissed it as an oddity of nature not worth considering. But Pratt had considered it—and used it. And he had blamed the predators and the winter kill for the cattle he had stolen.

Lee felt no elation as he mounted and turned back toward the house. He felt only an infinite weariness. Let Pratt steal and sell the cattle. If Iman knew where to look he could put all the pieces together. Lee grinned sardonically. Iman would appreciate that.

The rain slackened on the return trip. It didn't matter. He was as wet as he could be. Rain had trickled down the neck of his slicker and added to it was the natural sweating of the garment. He felt a sudden chill, and he sneezed against it. The clouds rifted to the west, and the upper half of the sinking sun shone for a while before it dipped out of sight. Usually, a clear red evening sun meant fair weather for the following day.

He wondered how far Pratt had gotten collecting his trail herd. The rain must surely have slowed him, but he would make all the haste he could. He wouldn't want to keep that herd held where anybody riding by might see it and ask questions. Lee shook his head. Who was going to ride by? Not Kate and surely not Newlin.

Lee thought, *Maybe he'll be ready to move tomor-*

row. If not, the following day. But whenever it was, Lee would be there at that narrow gash through the mountain for a week straight if necessary. He wanted to see that Circle A beef being driven through it. He wanted to close this book once and for all.

He frowned at the strange horse in the barn. He had a keen and practiced eye for a horse. He could see a man riding a horse just once and describe the animal a month later. This wasn't one of the Circle A horses—or if it was, he hadn't seen it before.

He walked around the horse. It was unbranded. He stood a moment in reflection, then shook his head. All he had to do to find out who owned this animal was walk into the house.

He hung up Amigo's gear and rubbed him down with a gunny bag. He stole some of the ranch's oats and fed the horse a generous measure. The ranch owed him those oats. By killing the bear he had saved enough future beef to more than repay the tiny cost of the grain.

He listened to the contented sound of Amigo's munching, and his face was sober. There wasn't going to be any future beef for Kate and her brother.

He walked to the kitchen, and his boots squished. His shirt clung clammily to his back, and he sneezed again. He felt a little light-headed and wished he had a stiff shot of whisky.

He stepped inside, and his jaw ridged. Homer Iman sat at the table drinking a cup of coffee. Two pairs of eyes exchanged unfriendly glances.

Lee glowered at him and said, "Just what I needed to ruin my day." He sneezed and flung up a hand to cover his nose.

Iman said, "You never did learn to bridle that tongue." He looked tired, as though he had spent a lot of hours in the saddle. Or maybe it was just old age reaching out and demanding its due.

Kate said tartly, "You look as though your day is already ruined." She resented his greeting to Iman. It showed in face and tone. "You'd better get out of those wet clothes before you catch cold."

"I never had a cold in my life." Lee was in a sour and perverse mood. He would take no advice, no help.

Iman said in disgust, "You never tell his kind a thing, Kate." He walked to the stove and poured himself a fresh cup of coffee.

He turned, and a mocking grin was on his face. "I'd offer you a cup, Mr. Dennis. But I just emptied the pot."

Lee had to throttle a desire to curse him. The stove was going, and the room should be warm. But he didn't feel any heat. An icy surge crept along his veins, and for a moment he thought his teeth were going to chatter.

Kate said, "I'll make another pot."

"He's not helpless," Iman growled.

Kate settled back uncertainly in her chair, looking questioningly from one to other.

Lee scowled at Iman and moved to the stove. He brewed a fresh pot of coffee, and his tongue told him how hot it was. But it couldn't do a thing against the chill in his body. It must be set deep in his bones to persist like this. He sneezed again, and poured himself another cup.

Kate turned her head, then said, "I thought I heard Newlin call. I'll fix you some supper when I get back."

Lee shook his head. "I'm not hungry." He picked up pot and cup and carried them to the table. He sat down across from Iman, and his teeth rattled against the edge of the cup. Something fast had moved in and seized him.

Iman seemed to watch him with a definite amount of pleasure. "I hope you caught your damned death of pneumonia," he said.

Lee did swear at him then—bitterly, with a sharpness born of the aching cold within him. Iman's face turned mottled red; he pointed a finger at Lee and said, "I've taken about enough of your fat lip. I know more than you think I—"

He broke off suddenly as Kate appeared in the doorway. Her troubled eyes went from one face to the other. "Homer," she said, and there was some kind of a plea in it.

Iman was in the grip of a runaway temper. It took great effort to pull his voice down short of a roar. He said, "Kate, you tell your smart new hand to watch every step he takes. The first wrong one, and I'll be snapping at his tail."

Lee's laugh was harsh and insulting.

Iman whirled on him. "Why, damn you," he said in wrath.

Kate laid a hand on his arm. "Please, Homer."

He stared at her a long moment, and regained control. He shook his head. "I haven't forgotten, Kate. But you're making a—" He broke off and sighed, then turned and left the room.

Kate stared at Lee with distinct dislike. "You work at it, don't you?"

He didn't understand her question, and he mumbled, "What?" The chills were getting worse. They came in waves, and each onslaught left an ache in his bones.

"Making people dislike you," she said coldly.

He heard her, but her voice seemed to come from such a long way off. He thought longingly of how whisky warmed a man. of how it dug deep and drove the last shred of cold out of his bones.

"Have you got any whisky?" he muttered.

She moved to him and laid the back of her hand briefly against his forehead.

"You're a sick man," she said. She moved to a cupboard and opened it. She pulled out a bottle of whisky and a glass.

He drank two water glasses full. All it seemed to do was make him more light-headed. His teeth still chattered.

She said crisply, "Get those wet clothes off and get in bed."

She was an Ashbaugh, and he didn't like her. He

113

stared at her, and his defiance faded. He turned and walked out of the room.

He got into bed, and it felt ice-cold. He hugged the blankets around him, and he couldn't stop shaking. He felt weak and listless, and it was difficult to get hold of a coherent thought. He seized on one thought, holding it desperately for fear it would escape him. He had to ride in the morning. He had to watch Pratt move cattle. Seeing that would end this job.

He was vaguely aware that she came into the room.

She said, "Here," and pulled the blankets from his fingers that clutched them around his neck. "Put this at your feet."

He took a heavy, warm object, and it took effort for him to figure what it was. She had heated a flat stone and wrapped it in cloth. His hands grabbed at the warmth eagerly. He pushed it down under the blankets and placed his feet on it.

She placed another heated stone on his chest and asked, "Better?" She put the blankets back in place and smoothed them out.

He wasn't sure whether or not he answered her. Everything seemed so hazy and far away. But a warmth was creeping into his body, and it brought a deep lassitude with it.

He spent a troubled night. Maybe he slept a little, but it seemed more like a drifting in and out of consciousness. He was aware that she came into the room several times. She replaced the stones when they cooled off, and a couple of times he felt hands lift him to shove the heated stones down under him. He thought vaguely about those hands. They couldn't have belonged to her. She didn't have that kind of strength. They had to be male hands, and he couldn't imagine who they belonged to. He got the past and the present all mixed up, and in the lucid moments he was afraid he babbled about both.

He fell into a deep slumber along about dawn. The last conscious thought that crossed his mind was that he had something to do today. He mustn't let anything stop him.

XIII

When he awakened the room was filled with shadowy light. He guessed it was the weak pre-dawning. In a few moments the light would strengthen and drive the shadows out. He felt weak and listless, but he was clearheaded enough.

He thought about getting up, and even made a tentative try. It took much more effort than he'd expected, and he sank back. He shook his head. He could lie here a few more minutes before he had to get up.

He must have had a restless night, for his head had been filled with troublesome dreams. He could put none of the sequences in a coherent pattern, but past and present spectres had wandered in and out of his dreams all night long.

He turned his head as the door opened. Kate and Iman came into the room.

Her eyes were drawn, and she was hollow-cheeked. Iman had the same weary cast to his face. Lee wondered about it, then dismissed it. They must have had something pretty engrossing to talk about if it had kept them sitting up most of the night.

She asked, "Do you feel better?" and that was an odd note in her voice. It sounded almost like anxiety.

He wanted no anxiety over him, and it harshened his voice. He said gruffly, "A lot better. I could eat a steer for breakfast."

Iman eyed him queerly. "What time do you think it is?"

Lee stared at Iman's expression. "Coming morning?" That expression caused him to make a question out of it instead of a statement.

"It's damned near night," Iman said. "After you hollered and yelled all last night you slept through most of today. You went into fever after the chills. She kept me running. I thought she was going to send me up into the mountains to get snow to pack you in." He grimaced at his bad joke. "You did a real good job of keeping both of us on our feet."

Lee knew a quick alarm. What he'd thought had been dreams had really been babbling. He asked tensely, "What did I talk about?"

"Just words," she said quickly. "None of it made sense."

116

He had the impression she was trying to reassure him, and he glanced from her to Iman's blank face. He could read nothing from either of their faces.

Something else hit him hard. He had lost an entire day. And Pratt had probably used that day to move the cattle. It really didn't make any difference if the cattle were gone. He would have to ride out there and check, then report back to Iman. But it wouldn't do any good to start now. Night would catch him before he was much more than out of sight of the house. The best he could do was leave in the morning.

Kate asked, "Do you feel like eating?"

He nodded. His stomach was a vast, rebellious hollow.

"I'll bring it in," she said.

He shook his head. He wanted no further favors from her. "I can walk into the kitchen," he said roughly.

Iman remained silent until she left the room. Then his face turned violent. "I've seen some ingratitude in my day—" He left it unfinished as he glared at Lee. "I'm going to tell you something. If you hurt her you can't ride far enough to get away from me. I'll run you right off the edge of the world."

"Oh, go to hell," Lee said wearily.

Iman's throat swelled, but he held the explosion. He spun on his heel and left the room.

Lee was surprised at how weak he felt. He spent effort in just dressing. She had cleaned and dried his garments, and he scowled at them. Had he asked her to do it?

He walked into the kitchen and sat down at the table. He didn't look at her. He didn't want to see any accusation in her eyes, and he felt sure it would be there. He had to keep spurring himself into righteous indignation to keep his anger alive. Had he asked her for special attention? Did a couple of kindnesses wipe out all the abuses of the past?

Iman sat across from him, a glitter in his eyes. Every time Lee glanced up that glitter fixed him like a knife point.

The ravenous reach of his hunger surprised even him. He ate a half-dozen fried eggs and a thick slab of ham. He pushed back his plate and sighed. He couldn't remember when a meal had tasted better.

He stood and looked at Kate. "Thank you," he said gruffly.

Her face was stiff, and she didn't meet his eyes. "It's all right."

He went back to his room and lay down fully dressed. He put his hands behind his head and stared at the ceiling. Pratt had probably moved the cattle today. *Isn't that what you wanted?* he growled to himself. Where was the satisfaction? Why was it all so flat and tasteless now?

He lay there wrestling with the devil of his problem, and he was losing. He paraded all the old, angry scenes through his mind, and he couldn't keep his grip on them.

Before midnight he knew it had whipped him. If the cattle were gone he would ride back and tell Iman. Iman could probably overtake Pratt before they were sold. Kate would get her cattle back and save her ranch. He growled aloud, "Will she?" and found a sorry satisfaction in the answer. She wouldn't —it was too big a job for her. But at least his wouldn't be the heavy hand that sent it toppling.

He lay there patiently waiting out the night hours. A man laid out his path and despite every effort it kept changing on him. He had come here filled with anger and hate, knowing that nothing could change or weaken that. But all of it was weakened now.

He slipped out of the house an hour before dawn. The night was chilly, and he shivered. Before he entered the barn, he looked back at the house. It was silent and dark. He smiled wanly. He was a man who liked to keep his accounts squared. By tomorrow night he wouldn't be in debt to her.

He saddled Amigo and led him a long way from the barn before he mounted. He swung into the saddle and headed north.

He kept Amigo at a smooth, even gait, and the miles fell behind him. When the dawn light was strong he wasn't too far from Pratt's camp.

He stopped and scanned the country behind him. He had the queer feeling that unseen eyes were upon him. He saw nothing moving and thought, *It's probably your conscience*. His lips moved in a bleak smile.

He picked up the reins, and Amigo started again. If the herd was gone it wouldn't be difficult to find its trail. He would follow it through the passage, then turn back to get Iman.

He stopped as a faint, far-off sound drifted to him. He heard it again, and there was no mistaking it this time. That was the bawling of cattle ahead of him, and they were still in the valley. It had taken longer than he'd expected for Pratt to make his gather.

The bawling was stronger and consistent now, the protest of cattle being forced in a direction they didn't want to go.

He put Amigo into a run and headed for high ground. He had no definite intentions other than watching Pratt drive the cattle out of the valley. The climb steepened, and he let the horse pick its own pace. He came out from between the trees, and the mountain face dropped off sheer before him.

He pulled the glasses from his saddle bag and focused them.

The drive was well under way, but riders still had to make quick dashes to turn back cattle reluctant at being driven from familiar ground. In a few miles the cattle would be more docile. But right now the riders sweated and cursed, keeping them in some semblance of a line.

He stared at the scene a long time, and a rage built in him that roared in his head. A jeering inner voice mocked, *Wasn't this what you wanted? Wasn't this what you were aiming for?*

No! he shouted at the voice in his mind. *Not like this. Not against a lone, helpless woman.* When a man was against a man it was different. But a man didn't fight a woman. The jeering voice wanted to make some other comments, but he swore at it. He'd changed his mind. That was all there was to it.

He threw a calculating glance at the terrain above him. He would have to climb high and then go down. But if he could reach that slash in the rock before Pratt did he could block the herd. He could stop Pratt without a head ever leaving the valley.

He looked at the herd again. It was beginning to string out. He wasn't going to have a lot of time. He would have to make it do.

XIV

He left Amigo on high ground and climbed down. He carried his rifle with him, and his jacket pockets were filled with bullets. It was rough, torturous going, and in places the rock was rotten, eroded by weather and time. Each time a piece crumbled under his boot or hand his heart blocked his throat. He was racing against time, and he couldn't race at all. He had to crawl, and it ate up the minutes.

He wouldn't let the need for haste force him into a too hasty move. He had the spot selected that he wanted to reach, a flat shelving big enough to lay down on, some hundred yards above the passage's floor. From it he'd be able to see the narrow opening, though the box canyon beyond it would still be blocked from his view.

He reached the shelf and lay down, squirming to find a more comfortable position. There were no soft spots in the rock. He had a naked and exposed position, but by pressing against the inner face his advantage of height would give him some protection. He didn't intend anybody to get through that opening to shoot at him, but if they did they would have an awkward angle of fire.

He listened and heard the wind soughing down the narrow slit. It seemed he lay there an eternity, and disturbing thoughts rode through his mind with sharp-tipped rowels. What if Pratt didn't use this exit —what if there was another one he didn't know about? He brushed the queasy fingers of doubt from his mind. Pratt had used this exit before—the dried manure was proof of it. And he would use it again.

He lifted his head as a faint sound carried to him. He listened with all his attention, and concluded his taut nerves had played him tricks. But that had sounded like cattle bawling.

Some of the tenseness went out of his face as he heard it again, closer now and leaving no doubt as to its source. The herd was coming. He had underestimated the distance Pratt had to drive, or else he had made much better time than he first expected.

He checked the mechanism of his rifle, working the lever until the magazine was empty, then wiping each bullet with thumb and forefinger before he reinserted it. The dry snicks of the lever were reassuring sounds. He aimed the muzzle at the narrow opening and squinted along the barrel. He would be shooting downhill, and he'd have to remember to compensate for it. He knew exactly how he was going to block that passage.

The waiting wasn't hard now, for they were coming. The bawling was stronger, rising in a concerted tide as the animals were forced into the box canyon. The riders would curse before they forced the leaders through that narrow opening, for cattle fought being pushed into something they couldn't see. Lee remembered an old trail boss' words: "Never try to swim cattle across a river if the sun is in their eyes. If they can't see the opposite bank you'll never get them across." In a way the same principle applied here. But once the first few were through the others would follow.

Just a little beyond him he could hear cattle and the loud voices of men. But here he was alone. The fact of it drove home hard at him, and he grimaced and snugged the rifle butt tighter against his shoulder.

He lay with aimed rifle, alert and anticipating the exact moment the first steer would appear, and still when it stuck its head through it surprised him.

It withdrew its head quickly, but it would reappear, for the riders would keep pressure on the rear cattle, forcing those in front on through.

The head appeared again, and the animal took a cautious step forward. It was literally forced along, and it bawled its protest at every grudging inch. Another head appeared at its flank, and two steers were all the passage would take.

Lee waited until the lead steer was halfway

through. He aimed between the eyes, and the rifle's report slammed back and forth between the rocky walls. The steer dropped in its tracks and never even kicked.

He swung the rifle muzzle and covered the second steer. It was trying to back out, but it couldn't move against the pressure behind it. Lee dropped it, and it fell partially on top of the first one. He put down the rifle and waited. He had the passage blocked with a wall of animal flesh. The next move was up to Pratt.

He heard the alarmed, yelled questions though he couldn't make out the words. Then Pratt's voice carried to him thin but clear.

"How the hell do I know who it is?" Pratt bellowed. "Put a rope on those steers and drag them out of the way."

Lee grinned bleakly. He'd change their minds for them.

The rifle butt came up again, and he waited. He saw the dim form of a man appear just behind the dead animals, and he had a rope in his hand. He didn't have enough room to swing a big loop, and he tried to dab the rope around the second steer's neck. Its head was bent at an awkward angle, and the man's swearing drifted up to Lee as he missed his first try.

He didn't get a chance at a second one. Lee put a bullet in his chest, and the man fell over backwards. Only his legs remained in view, and they were limply still.

Lee heard more swearing, and his teeth showed in

a bleak grin. Orrie sounded as though he were going crazy.

"Goddamnit," Pratt yelled. "How do I know who it is? But he's got us blocked. Get a rope on those steers so we can get at him."

Lee said softly, "You come and do it, Orrie."

He thought he saw a flitting shadow, but it was gone so quickly he couldn't be sure. Then a rope snaked out, but its loop missed.

Lee waited. The man would never make a successful cast from that far back. He would have to come closer, and if he did he'd show himself.

Another cast, then a third; they both missed. Pratt's swearing drove the man into moving nearer the steers. Lee caught a flash of face and a shoulder before they were withdrawn.

He waited patiently. He wanted more than just a flash to shoot at.

He saw the face again, and he squeezed the trigger. He heard a shrill yelp, and swore. The yell had had more fright than pain in it. At best he had only wounded the man or maybe nicked him with rock sliver. It would make them more cautious, and a good shot would be next to impossible.

The legs were still in view. At least he'd whittled a little on Pratt's force.

The cattle were still bawling, but they sounded farther back in the canyon. Pratt would let them go until he'd cleared the blockage of the dead steers. He wouldn't lose all his work of gathering the herd. One rider at the mouth of the canyon could hold them.

Lee heard Pratt yell again, and there was fear and frustration in it. He shouted an indistinguishable order, and a voice yelled in return, "I'm not getting my head blown off. You drag those steers out yourself, Orrie, if you want it done."

The silence grew heavy and oppressive, and the minutes were maddeningly slow in their march. Lee wished he could hear them yelling again. At least he would know where they were.

The rock grew harder with each passing tick of time. Would they give up this easily? He shook his head at the question. Pratt had come this far, and he knew he had to go all the way. Backing away from this would still ruin him. But what was he doing? Lee wished he knew.

Maybe Pratt was still figuring on some way to drag those steers clear. If he could do it and pour the herd through at a run he might make it. By now Pratt surely knew only a lone rifle was against him. And that rifleman would have much harder shooting at running animals.

Lee nodded. It seemed like sensible reasoning to him. Anyway all he could do was wait.

A pebble bounced down the steep slope, hit on Lee's shelf and arced on into the cut. His blood froze in his veins. He had left one thing out of his calculations, and it was going to cost him dear.

Now it wasn't hard to understand that long silence and wait. While he had watched the cut one or more of them had climbed above him. He was tempted to throw up his head and make a search, but that bouncing pebble said somebody was already over him. He rolled from the front edge of the shelf to the rear, and a bullet slammed into the space he had just left and wheeed off into space.

He tried to make himself infinitely small as he pressed against the juncture of shelf and wall. They had the high gun, and it was a deadly advantage.

Another slug ricocheted off the shelf, and he thought its angle was different from the first bullet. If so, there were two of them above him, and an already hopeless situation had worsened.

Another bullet plucked at his jacket sleeve. He had no doubt he was in plain view of them, and he felt as helpless as a fly without wings waiting for the foot to squash it. His flesh was drawn painfully tight. Maybe they would play with him, nicking at him with their shots before they slammed the fatal bullet home.

He heard another shot, and his eyes squeezed shut instinctively. Then he opened them. A man never heard the shot that hit him.

He heard a wild scrabbling overhead, and a waterfall of pebbles and rocks cascaded down around him. The scrambling and clawing went on for a few seconds longer, then Lee thought he heard a soft thump against the rocky wall. He dared to turn his head and look upward, and a body seemed to be falling straight at him. He pulled back as far as he could, and the body hit on the shelf's lip before bouncing out into space. Its arms and legs flopped grotesquely, and Lee knew the man was dead before he hit the floor.

He had another and fresher fear. Somebody was across the cut from him. He was bracketed from above and across. But he was discounting the falling body. That fall hadn't been an accident. A rifle slug had knocked the man from his lofty perch. Lee dared to hope. He didn't know who the man across from him was, but it could just be that he had help.

The thoughts didn't take the time of a breath before the rifle cracked again. Lee heard a long, keening yell, the sound of a man mortally hit. He saw another falling body, and this one didn't hit the shelf. It fell to the right of him in a long arc that ended with that thudding sound on the floor below.

A figure stood up from behind a rock across from Lee. He stared at it in disbelief. Sure he recognized Iman. He just couldn't believe it.

Iman pointed above Lee's head, then slashed his hand across in front of his face.

Lee got the meaning immediately. The men who had been shooting at him were all gone. He didn't have to worry any more.

He waved in return. He didn't know how or why Homer Iman was over there. He didn't care about the reasons. He said softly, "I'm obliged, Homer."

The expression of gratitude was followed by a thrust of resentment. Those had been agonizing moments while he had been under fire. Iman had to have seen it all. He'd taken his damned sweet time before he'd joined in.

You're complaining, Lee jeered at himself, and the resentment faded.

Iman was signaling again. He was motioning for Lee to climb down to the floor and go through the cut. Lee understood that. It took him longer to get that Iman was going to go high again and come down over the canyon.

Lee grunted. He knew what Iman wanted. He wanted to trap Pratt and the men in the canyon. Iman must have a hell of a lot easier going on his side than Lee did on his.

He waved his understanding and watched Iman begin an angling climb. He hoped Iman would be successful. If Iman made it in time he could cover Pratt and the rest from high ground while Lee came up from the rear.

He looked at Iman again before he began his descent. Iman was moving right along.

It took Lee ten minutes to climb down to the floor. The wall got pretty sheer at the last, and he had to search for a foot and hand hold. His arms and legs screamed at the strain he put on them. He dropped the last eight feet, trying to absorb the shock with bent knees. The floor of the cut slammed at him, and he went down.

He limped when he got to his feet. His knee had a twinge in it, and his hand was scraped. He looked up at the wall and shook his head. Only a damned fool would have tried to come down there.

He passed one of the men that Iman had shot off the wall, and the body was horribly battered. It lay face downward, and he felt nothing as he looked at it. He wasn't even curious enough to turn it over to see who it was.

He clambered over the dead steers in the passage and stepped into the wider canyon in time to hear Iman say, "Just hold it, you two. Or I'll take that restlessness out of you."

Iman stood above them, his rifle trained on them, and his face was hard and dispassionate. Ronders and Fleming cowered against the rocky wall of the canyon. Ronders had a shoulder wound, and blood seeped through the poorly tied handkerchief bandage. Their beaten, sullen look said they intended making Iman no trouble at all.

Iman glanced at Lee and growled, "It took you long enough."

Lee grinned. Iman could say anything he pleased.

Iman said, "Cover them until I get down."

Lee looked at the two men. "Where's Pratt?" he demanded.

He saw Fleming's lips twist in some quick anger, but neither man said anything. He didn't really expect that they would.

He waited patiently for Iman to join him. He couldn't hear any of the cattle bawling. Evidently the guard at the mouth must be gone, and the cattle had streamed back into the valley.

Iman came up moving stiffly, "That damned rock is hard," he complained.

"Where did you come from?" Lee demanded.

"Followed you when you left the house this morning. I lost you and wound up across from you." Iman allowed himself a brief grin. "I'd say it was lucky for you."

Lee stared at him. "Why were you following me?"

Iman snorted. "Did you think I didn't know you? I knew you the moment I laid eyes on you in town." He shook his head and sighed. "I'm getting to be the damndest liar. I didn't know you at all. Kate did. She told me about the burning. It wasn't hard to figure out why you were hard. I knew she was crazy to let you stick around, but she wouldn't listen to me. I hung around to keep an eye on you."

Some of the old bitterness came back. "You were keeping your eye on the wrong one."

"Was I?" Iman asked softly. "Remember me telling you a man picked his road. I just saw a man change his pick."

"I'm crazy," Lee said harshly.

Iman let it pass. "You could have asked for help and saved yourself a lot of trouble," he said mildly.

Lee's resentment returned. "It took you long enough to take a hand."

Iman sighed. "You never give anything away, do you? I had to wait and see which way it was going. Hell, I wasn't even sure what I was taking a hand in."

Lee admitted grudgingly that Iman couldn't have gone any other way. But his resentment was still there, and he switched its target.

"You didn't give us any help the night they burned us out," he said bitterly.

Iman's face remained patient. "I heard about the

burning a week after it happened. Nobody came in and made a complaint. Cleatis sure wasn't going to ride in and say, 'I did it.' "

Lee had to admit the fairness of that. Iman was kicking at all of the props that had held him up for so many years.

Iman saw the warring emotions in his face. "It's kinda hard for a man to get all the hate out of his system."

Lee said wearily, "There wasn't much left to fight. Just Pratt. I found out he's been stealing from her. At first I wasn't going to do a thing about it. Then I couldn't stand to see her broken that way."

"She thinks something of you too." Iman grinned at Lee's glare. "You're too stiffnecked to see or admit anything. I never saw a woman worry more when you were sick. If it had happened to me I'd have been able to figure out something from it."

Lee couldn't get hold of a clear thought. He didn't think anything of Kate—not the way Iman was suggesting. He couldn't make the denial as strong as he thought it should be.

"You might be surprised at what would happen if you gave people a chance," Iman said. "If it was me I'd do a little worrying about her right now. Pratt's gone. He could be heading straight back to the house. He might be figuring to use her as his one chance to get out of the country safely. Newlin sure as hell isn't going to stop him."

He nodded gravely at the startled flash in Lee's

face. "One of us has got to bring these two in. Do you want me to ride to the house?"

"I'll do it," Lee snapped.

Iman said dryly, "I kinda thought you would."

Lee ran for the two horses ahead of them. They were ground-reined, and he wouldn't waste any time catching one of them up. He picked the roan. It was long-legged, and the deep chest said it had endurance. He had a long, hard ride ahead of him, and he needed both speed and endurance. Iman was dredging up unnecessary fears. Pratt wouldn't go back there—not after this had happened. But still, he might. The chance of it put a hard hand around Lee's heart.

XV

Pratt heard the first shots, and a wicked grin spread over his face. He expected it to be followed by a yell of triumph from the men he had sent to get above the unknown rifleman, but it didn't come. A frown took over the grin. The frown deepened when he heard the third report. Both of his men carried carbines, and he knew the crack they made. That third shot had had a more solid sound, the sound of a larger calibered rifle.

The bigger rifle sounded again, and it was followed by a yell that tore at Pratt's guts. That was Hurley's yell, and it carried the pain of a man mortally hit.

He was certain Hurley wasn't coming back. Had that first shot gotten Red? He hadn't heard Red cry out. But that meant nothing. Pratt had seen men so hard hit there wasn't enough strength left in them to push out a grunt. He'd better figure that both Hurley and Red were gone. And Burl had been killed when he'd tried to put a loop on one of the dead steers.

He cursed savagely to dispel the little shiver that ran through him. He had been so damned close to success; all he'd had to do was string the herd out along the cut and push them on through it. Then somebody had stopped him cold, blocking the passage by dropping two steers. Pratt had figured that rifleman to be sitting high enough to be looking down at the floor of the cut, and he had sent Hurley and Red to climb above him. The waiting had been tough. When he'd heard the carbine shots he'd thought he'd won. Now he didn't know where he stood. He had ridden in here with five, and now he could only figure on a positive figure of two left. And Ronders had a chunk gouged out of his left shoulder. He didn't know who was back there in that cut, but whoever it was was deadly.

He swallowed hard. One man couldn't have done all that damage. He had to have help. But how much help? That was the fearful question that was driving him wild. If there were two men back there in that cut the odds were about even—he couldn't count on much from Ronders with that bad shoulder. If there were more than two men back there he was outnumbered, and that scared hell out of him.

Ronders said, "Orrie, my shoulder hurts like hell." He tried awkwardly to tie his neckerchief about the wound with one hand.

"Shut up," Pratt screamed at him. "I'm trying to think."

Had Iman gotten wind of this somehow and brought a posse with him? If so there would be men waiting at the mouth of the canyon, and he was trapped. He turned the problem over from every angle. He hated to give Iman credit for that many brains. And surely Fleming, the man he had sent back to hold the cattle in the canyon, would have notified him in some way. If there had been a fight out there, wouldn't he have heard the shots?

Indecision was driving him crazy, and he had to do something. He could at least check and see if the mouth of the canyon was still open.

He moved to Ronders and roughly tied the neckerchief in place. "I'm going back and see if Fleming is having any trouble."

Ronders' eyes were scared. "Orrie, what do you think is happening?"

Pratt wanted to lash him across the face. That was the question that was pulling him to pieces.

"Nothing," he said. "You keep an eye on that opening. If the bastard steps into the canyon, drop him."

Ronders said dubiously, "Maybe there's more than one of them. Shouldn't we have heard from Hurley and Red by now?"

So he hadn't recognized Hurley's yell. He didn't know that Hurley and probably Red were dead. Ronders never was able to figure out very much by himself.

Pratt said, "You stay here like I told you."

He mounted and turned his horse. He wanted to put it into a gallop, but that would never do. His teeth bared in a merciless grin. If everything was clear at the mouth of the canyon he was going to send Fleming back here. Ronders and Fleming would hold back whatever was against him. And he would have his start.

The cattle were packed near the mouth of the canyon, and Fleming was the cork holding them from scattering back into the valley. The sight of Fleming was all the assurance Pratt needed. Nothing had happened out here.

Pratt rode through the milling animals, cursing and kicking at them. He made his way to Fleming, and the man was angry and scared.

"What the hell's going on?" he yelled. "I've been working my butt off trying to hold them." His eyes were apprehensive. "What was all that shooting?"

"We got the bastard that was holding us up," Pratt grunted.

"Who was it?"

"Dennis. Hurley and Red picked him off the wall."

Fleming's eyes were round. "Then he was an Association man," he said. "You had it figured right, Orrie. What's going to happen now?" His voice was still tight.

"By the time they send somebody else we'll have the cattle sold and be long gone. Get on back there and give Ronders a hand dragging those dead steers clear. I'll hold the cattle."

Fleming didn't argue about it. He moved back into the canyon, and Pratt watched him until he was out of sight. He wondered if it *had* been Dennis—no, Lee Martin—who had held them up. It could have been. Martin had been snooping around for something. But it didn't figure at all. Didn't Martin hate the Circle A? He should have thrown in with them.

There was no use crying over it now, and Pratt pushed it from his mind. He had some money cached back of the bunkhouse. The best thing he could do was get it and clear out of this country. He had a moment's regrets for all his lost dreams. And his guts twisted at the thought that he wouldn't see Kate again.

He dwelt on the thought of her, and his eyes narrowed. Sure, why not? He could take her with him. Her presence would insure his safety until he got far away. That bleak grin showed on his face again. She wouldn't want to go, but that wouldn't make any difference. He was going to salvage more out of this than he had at first thought.

He rode hard until he came within sight of the buildings, then slowed his pace the rest of the way in. If anybody saw him coming they wouldn't be able to guess by his manner that he had anything more on his mind but routine matters.

If Kate saw him from the house she didn't come to the door. He had a quick worry that she had gone someplace, but a quick look in the barn reassured him. Her horse was still here.

He saddled the animal, led it outside and tied it to the side of the corral that was out of sight from the house. He moved to the rear of the bunkhouse and dug up the tin can. He pulled a thick wad of bills from it. The regret came back momentarily. It could have been a lot more. It could have been all the land he was looking at.

He swore at the regret and thrust the money into his pants pocket. He turned and walked toward the house.

He moved noiselessly into the kitchen, and he could hear voices coming from the front room. He eased to the door and listened.

"Talk to me, Newlin," Kate said, and there was impatience and something more in her voice.

Newlin said sullenly, "What can I talk about? What do I know sitting here day after day?"

Pratt's lips curled in contempt. Newlin wasn't worth feeding to keep alive. If that accident had happened to Cleatis the old man would have ridden that wheel chair bellowing his defiance to his dying day. Even Kate had a lot more spunk than her brother.

Kate said, "Newlin, I know something's happened. Everybody's gone, and I can't find out a thing."

The sullenness remained in Newlin's voice. "I don't know what I can do about it."

Pratt stepped into the room.

Her eyes widened, and her voice had a ragged tear. "Orrie, is something wrong?"

He felt a quick and senseless anger at her. Maybe none of this would have happened if she hadn't let Martin stay around. She'd known who he was from the moment she'd hired him. She must have felt something for him. Pratt's face twisted with jealousy. He could find out in a hurry.

"Martin's dead," he said brutally. "I caught him trying to rustle your cattle."

Her eyes closed, and her face went white. She didn't say an audible word, but Pratt was sure she breathed a violent, *"No!"*

Newlin swung puzzled eyes to Pratt. "Martin?"

"Lee Martin," Pratt jeered. "The kid of the homesteader we burned out. You ought to remember him. You were there. He's growed up now. He came back to get even with you."

Kate's eyes were open again, and color returned to her face.

"I don't believe you," she said steadily.

Her reactions told Pratt everything he wanted to know, and his face flamed. "I shot him," he said savagely.

She shook her head in a stubborn gesture. "I don't believe you. Homer was suspicious of him too. I know he was watching him. If you'd killed him like you said, Homer would have been close around. Why isn't he here with you?"

Pratt had his answer as to the identity of the men who had stopped him. Iman and Martin. She must have set them on him. He took a long stride toward her, and his hand lifted. It took quite a struggle not to let the blow go.

She didn't flinch at the threat. "You were stealing from me, Orrie, weren't you? They found out about it. And you're running now."

He was in control of himself again, and he said with hard amusement, "You're too damned smart for your own good, Kate. I had big plans. I could've run all this for you. But you wouldn't look at me."

He saw the revulsion in her face, and it almost snapped the thread of his control.

She said quietly, "Orrie, I think you've gone crazy."

"Maybe," he agreed. "You're right about one thing. I'm running. And you're going with me."

The contempt was naked in her face. "Get out of here," she said coldly.

He could overpower her and carry her out, but that would take a struggle. There was an easier way, and it sat in the wheel chair.

Newlin hadn't uttered a word. He sat with his jaw sagging and his eyes bugging out. Pratt thought, *Maybe his mind's affected too. He doesn't look as though he knows what's going on.*

He stepped to the side of the wheel chair and lashed the back of his hand into Newlin's face. The blow rocked Newlin's head to the right. It pulled his body that way, and a wheel of the chair rose. It would have overturned if Pratt hadn't slammed a hand against its arm, knocking it back to the floor.

"Are you going, Kate?" he asked softly.

Newlin's eyes watered, and the corner of his mouth bled. He raised a hand to the hurt, then looked at the smear of blood on it. His eyes looked more dazed than ever.

"How much of it do you think he can take?" Pratt asked. "I can stand here and beat him to a pulp."

He raised his hand again, and the hating in her face gave him a wicked pleasure. That kind of hating could be broken and turned into something interesting.

"Make up your mind," he said.

She looked like a trapped animal as her eyes swept the room. They rested on the rifle hanging over the mantel, and her hope was plain.

"You'd never make it," Pratt said.

She saw it too. He was a couple of steps closer to the rifle than she was. Her eyes went dead, and there was a noticeable sagging about her.

"I'm tired of waiting," Pratt said, and slashed his hand again into Newlin's face.

He let the chair go over this time, and it spilled Newlin out near the fireplace.

She cired out in anguish. "Don't! I'll go."

"That's better," Pratt said.

He glanced carelessly at Newlin. The man wasn't all dead, for there was hating in his eyes as malignant as any Pratt had ever seen. That kind of hating would eat a man up, for he couldn't do a damned thing about it. The thought tickled him, and he grinned.

"Move out, Kate," he ordered.

She went out of the door ahead of him.

He glanced back at Newlin before he left the room. Newlin was struggling to get up, and it amused Pratt to watch him for a moment. Newlin would never make it. If somebody didn't come back and help him he'd lay there and rot.

The room was very still after they'd gone. Newlin's struggles turned his neck cords into stiff ropes, and his face was twisted with the bitterness of his fight. He got his fingers hooked around the rough edges of the stones in the fireplace and dragged himself erect an inch at a time. His face was an anguished mask by the time he got his elbows propped on the mantal. He was bathed in sweat, but his eyes held a triumphant blaze. He had made it this far; he had stood alone. He reached up and removed the rifle from its rack, and his hands were shaking so much he was afraid he'd drop it.

He looked at the door, and it was a monstrous distance from where he stood. Oh God, he'd never make it. It had taken him so long just to get this far. By the time he reached the door Pratt would be gone.

He looked at the overturned wheelchair. If he could right it he could use it to get to the door. He tried, but he couldn't reach it without letting go of the mantel. He was afraid he'd fall again, and getting back to his feet would take more time.

He worked his way along the mantel, his teeth locked against the tremendous struggle it was taking, his face haggard with the strain.

From the mantel he could reach a window, and he clawed his way along the top of the bottom pane. He cursed his useless legs as he forced his arms to drag them along.

The long oak table near the window gave him his next support. He reached the end of it, shaking all over. It had taken him an eternity to reach this far. He wasn't going to make it, and he sobbed his despair.

His head lifted at the sound of scuffling outside, then he heard Pratt growl, "You try to run again on me, Kate, and I'll slap your head off. Do you want it that way?"

Newlin couldn't hear his sister's reply, but Pratt's words put new hope in him. Kate had evidently made a break for it, and it had taken Pratt time to catch and drag her back. He was still out there.

Newlin had a good three feet to go to reach the door, and there was no support for him. He had to lunge for it, and if he missed the door he would crumple into a worthless heap.

Ten minutes ago he would have cried out in terror at the impossibility of such a task. Now the white-hot hating in him gave him the strength and ability to make the try.

He held the rifle in his left hand and straightened,

laying the rifle along the table for support. He drew a deep breath, and his face was a death's mask.

He lunged for the doorknob and caught it in his right hand. He teetered for a terrible moment and thought he would go down, but the hand held against the sagging weight of his body.

He dragged himself to the doorjamb and leaned against it. He breathed in hard, hungry gasps, and sweat bathed his face. Pratt was still trying to subdue Kate, and Newlin couldn't shoot for fear of hitting her.

He fought the awful weakness that was draining him and put the rifle to his shoulder.

"Let her go, Orrie," he called. "Or I'll blow your head off."

Pratt whirled, still holding Kate. He held her in front of him, and he said in amazement, "I'll be God-damned."

The sight of the rifle put no fear in him. Newlin was too weak, and the rifle muzzle wavered in eccentric circles. It was a miracle the man had gotten as far as he had. And now he was too weak to hold the rifle steady.

"Newlin," Kate cried, fear and wonder in her voice. "Newlin."

Pratt's left arm was an iron band holding her tightly against him. He drew his pistol with the other hand and said, "Newlin, drop the rifle—or I'll shoot her."

The blaze in Newlin's eyes weakened and went out. The last of his strength was gone. He couldn't keep the rifle from sagging, and he couldn't shoot. His cry had mortal pain in it as he let the rifle fall.

"That's real smart," Pratt said approvingly.

XVI

Lee had picked well in his mount. He set it to a savage pace, and it responded. Reasoning returned to him after the first burst, and he let the horse slow. Killing him off in the first couple of miles wouldn't do him any good—not with all the miles he had to make. After that first spurring he didn't touch the animal again. He was an honest horse, and he gave willingly. Lee could only sit here while his thoughts raced far ahead of him. How much of a start did Pratt have? Was he at the house already? Those kind of thoughts could drive a man crazy, and he tried to take his mind off them. Maybe Iman was crazy. Maybe Pratt wouldn't even go near the house. That one didn't give him too much consolation. Against the terrible urgency that Iman might be right the last thought weakened and faded.

He was punishing himself with worry, and it wasn't doing a damned bit of good. He had so many miles to make, and it would take so much time. He faced the ultimate thought squarely. If Pratt had taken Kate with him, if he had harmed her in any way, Lee would follow him and kill him. He made it a harsh, bitter fact, and he seized on it to strengthen him.

He came in sight of the house, and it looked strangely quiet. His heart sank as he saw no sign of activity anywhere about it. Then he saw the two horses tied to the corral. He put the glasses on them and recognized them. One was Pratt's, the other Kate's. Pratt was still here. He must be in the house. If he was there Kate was with him, and she had only Newlin to protect her. Newlin couldn't do a thing about stopping anything Pratt wanted to do.

Lee put the barn between himself and the house and came in fast. He jumped off and dropped the reins. The two horses were still tied, and he jerked his gun from its holster. He had to be careful now. If Pratt saw him and holed up in the house he would be hard to dig out. For Lee couldn't shoot at him without endangering Kate and Newlin.

He came around the barn and looked at the back door of the house. The brooding silence surrounding the house held. He was faced with a terrible problem. He had two doors to watch, and which should he choose? If he picked wrong Pratt could use the other one. Lee knew he wouldn't be able to wait long under the strain of the escaping minutes. Kate was in there with him.

His head lifted as he thought he heard scuffling and the sound of a voice from the front of the house. He hurried around the house and stopped by the front corner. Pratt held Kate against him. Lee heard Pratt say, "Drop the rifle, Newlin—or I'll shoot her."

The picture was laid out before Lee, but it was hard to believe. Newlin leaned against the doorjamb, trying to train a wobbly rifle muzzle on Pratt. It wasn't possible to believe, but he must've come this far unaided.

Lee was close enough to Kate's brother to hear the hollow groan deep in his throat. Then he dropped the rifle and slid down the door facing to the porch floor. The despair on his face was tragic. He had given so much to get this far.

"That's real smart, Newlin," Pratt approved.

"He's smarter than you are, Orrie," Lee said calmly.

Pratt's grunt was the sound an animal made when it was surprised, half anger and half panic. He whirled, trying to put his full attention on Lee and hold Kate at the same time. He was successful at neither. She jerked free and ran a few stumbling steps before she fell.

Lee's eyes were riveted on Pratt's face. He saw the ashen fading of the man's color, saw the eyes glassy with effort as he tried to swing his gun around.

Lee shot him in the chest. Pratt staggered back and coughed hard. Several flecks of blood appeared at his lips. His gun hand was heavy, and sweat washed his forehead as he struggled to raise it.

Lee shot him again. The man had tremendous vitality. He staggered in broken steps, his weight slamming down on his heels. But his upper body was bending forward, and his eyes were beginning to glaze.

Lee shot him for the last time. His face was coldly dispassionate as he watched Pratt's bending pick up speed. He hadn't needed the second or third shot, but had used them anyway. Perhaps it was a working off of the hating of the past.

Pratt fell on his face. One hand flopped a little, then he was still.

Lee turned to Kate. He wanted to ask her if she was all right, but she was already on her feet and running toward the porch.

Tears streamed down her face as she cried, "Newlin, are you hurt?"

His face held a weary joy. "I made it out here, Sis. I had to do it." He tried to rise, and his arms wouldn't support him. His face turned apologetic. "I guess you'll have to help me back. I'm tuckered out."

Lee brushed by Kate. He picked up Newlin and carried him inside. He waited until Kate righted the wheel chair, then put Newlin in it. His throat was tight, and a smarting was behind his eyes. He felt a tremendous awe of this man. He had done the impossible.

"Newlin," he started gruffly, but then he couldn't go on.

Newlin looked at him, and the weariness couldn't wash the radiance from his face. "I was the only one here," he said simply. "I had to try and stop him." His eyes looked at a glory that no one could understand unless they had sat in that chair for a long time. "And I'll do it again."

Lee's hand rested briefly on his shoulder. No one

could doubt the force behind Newlin's voice. "Sure you will," he said roughly.

Kate stared at him with a queer intensity. "Will you stay, Lee? We need you."

At his surprise, she smiled wistfully. "Yes, I knew you. I knew you the moment you came here. You see, I never forgot you."

His mind raced ahead to all that had to be done. The ranch didn't even have a crew. But it was spring, and the new grass would hold the cattle fast until a new crew could be hired. With the draining of its life's blood stopped, the Circle A could be put back on its face. Some of the bitter cast to his face was fading, and the flicker of a smile was in his eyes. That crusty old Iman was smarter than Lee had given him credit for. A man did pick his road.

She misread his silence and said fiercely, "Do you have to go on hating? Cleatis and Pratt are dead. Newlin didn't want to go that night—Cleatis made him. Who's left for you to hate?"

He smiled at her, and the harsh burden of a dozen years dropped from his shoulders. "Kate," he said gently, "I was just trying to find the words to ask you to let me stay."

Her eyes smiled through the tears. They told him so many things; they gave him a clear and shining promise of the future. He'd never ride a lonely road again.

The Biggest, Boldest, Fastest-Selling Titles in Western Adventure!

CHARTER'S MOST WANTED LIST

Elmer Kelton
__15266-X	DONOVAN	$2.50
__08396-X	BUFFALO WAGONS	$2.50
__06364-0	BITTER TRAIL	$2.50

Frank Bonham
__07876-1	BREAK FOR THE BORDER	$2.50
__77596-9	SOUND OF GUNFIRE	$2.50

Giles A. Lutz
__34286-8	THE HONYOCKER	$2.50
__88852-6	THE WILD QUARRY	$2.50

Will C. Knott
__29758-7	THE GOLDEN MOUNTAIN	$2.25
__71146-4	RED SKIES OVER WYOMING	$2.25

Prices may be slightly higher in Canada.

---

27 million Americans can't read a bedtime story to a child.

It's because 27 million adults in this country simply can't read.

Functional illiteracy has reached one out of five Americans. It robs them of even the simplest of human pleasures, like reading a fairy tale to a child.

You can change all this by joining the fight against illiteracy.

Call the Coalition for Literacy at toll-free **1-800-228-8813** and volunteer.

Volunteer Against Illiteracy.
The only degree you need is a degree of caring.